RAJ VIJAY

The Flipside Cult

First edition

This book was professionally typeset on Reedsy.
Find out more at reedsy.com

Contents

Preface

What if everything we consume—news, jobs, relationships, even dreams—was never really ours to begin with? What if it was all orchestrated? By the invisible rhythm of consumerism—the quiet puppeteer of our modern lives.

The Flipside Cult is not just a novel; it is a question, asked too late, in a world too noisy to hear it. Born from the union of logic and longing, this story follows a genius—Neil Sengupta, a quiet storm of a woman—Apanna, a karmic monk in disguise—Arjun, and the rooted rebel—Veera. Together, they build a tool. Not a weapon. Not a utopia. A mirror. A mirror that reflects not just society's structures, but also the surrogate freedom, consumerism, and the price we silently pay for it. This book moves across cities, countries, and hearts. It begins in a jail cell and ends in courtrooms and living rooms, where revolutions are born not in shouts, but in subtle realizations. You may call it dystopian fiction. I call it our quiet reality.

This story is for the thinkers who whisper when the world shouts. For the rebels who code, question, and cry. For those who have always felt that something is not quite right.

Welcome to *The Flipside Cult*.

You may never see the world the same way again.

Acknowledgments

Writing *The Flipside Cult* has been a journey of not just words, but emotions, questions, courage, and companionship. This book could never have taken shape without the unwavering presence and support of a few extraordinary people in my life.

To **Rachana Vyas**, my first reader and my most patient listener. Thank you for being the calm in my creative storm. Your thoughtful reflections gave me the strength to keep writing when I doubted the story, and myself.

To **Heena M Shrivastava**, for your sharp editorial insight and honest publishing guidance. You held the story up to a mirror and helped me see its best version. I owe much of the book's polish to your gentle yet firm advice.

To **Tanya Singh,** for sharing a close connection with the book and letting my creative side uncover the stories buried deep inside the pieces of paper.

To my late father, **Hanuman P. Vijayvargiya**, whose belief in me never wavered. Your words, like quiet torches, lit the darkest tunnels of doubt. Your firm motivation has kept my writing spark alive since the very beginning. Your presence never faded!

To my mother, **Kailashi Devi**, whose prayers to Lord Shiva are the invisible threads that bind our family of six siblings together. Your blessings are woven into every page of this book.

To my wife, **Aditi**, for being my anchor. Your love, patience, and strength helped me balance this creative pursuit with life's responsibilities. Thank you for believing in this dream even when it pulled me away from everything else.

To my little princess, **Adira**, whose Midas touch melted the big rock of inaction and converted a writer into an author!

And to **Lord Ganesha** for blessing me with such amazing life experiences and being with me at the time of need, ALWAYS!

This novel is a piece of my heart. But it carries the fingerprints of all of you.

With love and deepest gratitude,

Raj Vijay

1

Love and Freedom

"Your parents are here to receive you."

Apanna woke up, lifting her unsteady head from a wooden table, swirling and bursting with a hangover. One glance around the eight-by-eight room gave her a glimpse of sunlight streaming through the ventilator.

She squinted her eyes and tried to squeeze out the last memory from her sloshed-out head. Almost eight hours ago was the last conversation with Veera and Arjun. Some questions lingered like an uncovered grave. Why did Neil not join the call? The one she wanted to talk to the most. They said that Neil had some work, but she knew him. He would not have missed that call, and she was sure something was not right last night.

She put her head down on the table again and closed her eyes.

"Oh, I was put in a lock-up," she murmured to herself, and her mind began to repeat the last night in her dreams.

*

"Ms. Apanna Popat. Arrest warrant against you."

Half asleep and half awake, she muttered, "Ok, so what?"

"You will get into the van, ma'am, and will be jailed until bail is granted."

It was almost like a dream coming true. Arrests always make big headlines. She put a smile on her face, went into her house, took her bag, and hopped into the police jeep.

She had always imagined police stations to look like the ones in Bollywood movies. But here, no prostitutes were sitting on the tables, no chaiwala wandering around, no money being exchanged under the table, no *khaini* chewing. She wondered whether she was really in a police station.

She was respectfully led to the inspector-in-charge of the station. "Please take a seat, ma'am."

"Thank you, ma'am." Apanna had not expected to see a woman in her early 20s as the inspector-in-charge. She thought she would meet a rowdy policeman with the 'Singham' moustache and a revolver lying on the table. A girl in that seat was the least she could expect.

The in-charge looked at Apanna carefully and then signalled the constable to put her in the lock-up in the last corner.

"No questions asked? Did she just check me out?" Apanna thought and followed the constable.

"I need water," said Apanna to the constable, settling herself down on a chair placed in the middle of the room.

"Ok, ma'am." The constable bowed and left the room.

The excitement of being arrested just started taking a U-turn for Apanna. She expected rounds of questions being thrown at her in a small, dark room, a spotlight on her face, a third degree! The least she got was a girl in her 20s checking her out!

And then she saw a ray of hope.

The inspector-in-charge entered with a glass of water in one hand and a newspaper in the other.

She put the newspaper in front of Apanna and stared at her.

Now it felt like a police station. Apanna finished her glass of water and put on her glasses.

" **'The Flipside Cult: Our War Against Ourselves.'** Do you want me to read the whole article, or is this enough?" asked Apanna.

"I guess neither of us needs to read further, as you have written it, and I have read it. Damage has been done, Apanna, and clearly, the engine is a sociopathic product," said the inspector-in-charge with a concerned voice.

"It does not violate any internet laws. It is the power of the free internet. It is your personal opinion that it is a sociopathic product." Apanna looked right into her eyes.

Avani Bharadwaj, the inspector-in-charge, apprised Apanna calmly. With short, curly hair, a pair of full-rimmed round spectacles sitting on a sharp nose, and arched brows, Apanna looked like a girl in her late teens, trying to project herself with an air of confidence and candidness.

Avani took the newspaper and started reading a highlighted portion. "Brilliance Industries and 20 other blue-chip stocks fell by 40 percent. Seven top executives from different firms resigned on the same day. BBC is calling it the event of the millennium for the Indian stock market."

"Yes. It sounds like one," Apanna said indifferently.

"And still you are not moved? You guys have created a destructive internet tool; isn't it clear yet?"

"Of course, I do mourn for the shattered economy. But I guess the Cult is not doing anything illegal or immoral. Information and awareness are crucial for the centralization of wealth among a tiny portion of the population, and for the rest, consumerism is the only driving force. The engine is just trying to expose the roots of consumerism. How deeply they go! Everybody in the population has power, and the Cult is just uniting that power against the few privileged ones."

"So outspoken, you JNU folks! Illegal or immoral, the session court has banned the engine, and the public will not be able to make any meaningless conclusions around the 'flipside theory' and spread it across social media. I hope no more harm will be done. Your bail has also been granted. You will be released in the morning."

Apanna leaned forward, staring at Avani, took the newspaper, and adjusted her spectacles.

*

Apanna left the police station with her parents, her head still foggy from the vodka.

She was surprised to find that her parents had been informed last night only about her arrest, and they arranged her bail. Now they were at the police station to pick her up! Probably, her house help informed them, but this was the least of her concerns. Her whole focus was on the last night's call and Neil's absence.

Apanna sat in the back seat in her father's car beside her mother, while her mother grabbed her hand tightly. This was the same grip with which her mother dragged Apanna to her room and locked her up without food for a day for every small mistake she made in high school. Words would start banging her eardrums, even before they spurted out of her mother: *Look at your hair! Did you cut it on your own? Why do you wear these crop tops? Delhi is not a safe place.* Everything ended with the usual question, which was more of a declaration and threat: *Who is going to marry a girl like you?*

But shockingly, her mother was quiet today. So was her father. Almost a sure sign that either her arrest had hurt her parents to their core, or the 'Flipside Cult' had done damage that she would be proud of, but the society they live in won't be!

She looked out of the window. Every advertisement hoarding seemed fake to her, just an agent of consumerism. She had been with the Flipside Cult for over two years, and it still exploded her veins how the whole system made the society its consumer.

She was so lost in her thoughts that she did not realize her father had taken the car on Rajpath and was pulling in front of the PM's office.

"Woah, Papa. Am I being counselled by the PM now?" She taunted.

Her father was in no hurry to answer. They showed the temporary gate pass and entered the PMO. There were many people waiting in the lobby. The faces were easily identifiable. Top industrialists, top politicians, top social workers.

"Why do I have a feeling that they know me?" whispered Apanna to her father.

They were soon called to meet the PM.

They entered the PMO. As soon as they entered the office, the PM asked her to take a seat and her parents to give them some alone time.

"Good morning, sir. It's a pleasure to meet you."

"It's a pleasure to meet young energies like you, too, Ms. Popat."

"And to keep them in jail, too, Mr. PM?"

"Energies cannot be jailed, young lady. Especially, the younger ones. I consider society a total failure if it does not provide enough space to its young minds. Your space is out there, that's why you are free." He smiled.

"Out there is a safe and beautiful illusion, sir. We tried to introduce the reality, and it backfired."

"I like your boldness." He smiled.

"Let me tell you something about the Sun and the Moon. The Sun is powerful. Very powerful, Ms. Popat. It has a self-sustaining system of generating energy. By the way, this is what I read in my primary classes, so no rocket science here. The Moon shines for a different reason, though. It relies on the sunlight for its own brightness. However, to most people, both carry their glory independently. Now you tell me how foolish and unwise it is for the Moon to try to destroy the Sun and still keep glowing? It will never succeed, and even if it does, will it carry its glow?" asked the PM with an intense look.

Apanna was looking straight into the PM's eyes. Was he trying to demotivate her? All she could get was that he referred to the current system as the Sun and The Flipside Cult as the Moon. Or was he referring to the top tycoons and politicians as the Sun?

"Ms. Popat?"

"Yes, sir, noted. But you know the Cult has been banned, and today can be considered the night of no moon." She gave a faint smile.

"Neil Sengupta has been found dead," the PM said.

This was something that Apanna was not expecting even in her wildest dreams. The following silence was loud in her ears, a never-ending shriek of shock that left her stoned for a moment. Time seemed to stop. No, this could not happen.

She looked up at the PM, unable to decipher what he was saying. Something started running from her guts and through her entire body. She was shrinking. The PM offered her a glass of water. She shook her head.

"Look, Ms. Popat, the damage has been done, and the court has done its job to ensure stability. The Flipside Cult is banned in India. You have a bright future as a journalist. Please focus on your career."

Apanna left the room, numb and devastated.

*

She took a long breath and closed her eyes as the car crossed India Gate.

"We heard about Neil, and we are very sorry." Apanna's mother put her hand on her head.

Apanna turned to her mother, trying to look strong for a while, but then burst out crying.

Her father was looking through the back mirror. He wiped his tears away and said, "Daughter, be strong. The war against consumerism, which Neil started, you have to lead and win! Don't let Neil become your weakness, but strength."

He tried his best to console his devastated daughter. But the inner visuals and voices of Neil almost retarded Apanna's outer senses. She was in no state to be consoled. All she wanted was to submerge into the deep layers of her mind where Neil still resided, in his full, lively image. She closed her eyes and started thinking about the journey with Neil.

*

In her final year at college, she was among five other students chosen for an exchange program at MIT Media Lab in the US. Neil was her mentor there, a postgraduate student in the Computer Science department. She was smitten the very first time she met Neil. A tall, Bengali guy with light brown eyes. His hair matched the colour of his eyes. Full-sleeved, round-necked T-shirts suited his physique. He had an average build and a beautiful smile. To Apanna, he was PK from *To All the Boys I've Loved Before*, and she herself was Jean.

Will I ever be able to tell him that I have a crush on him? used to be her bedtime thought, leading to a dreamland shared with him every night.

She liked the United States, too. It was a big cultural change for her. She could laugh her heart out without some aunty pointing it out; she could work with flexible hours, not necessarily from 10–5 with her college life, and she could wear anything she liked without being eve teased and judged. But what she liked the most was Neil's company. It was an instant connection she felt for him. She had a strong feeling that Neil was also into her.

Is it love at first sight? Will I go back to India without confessing, or will there come a day when either of us would propose? She used to wonder.

Neil usually stayed until late at night in the lab. It was a Friday, and since she did not have any plans, Apanna decided to stay with Neil and help him.

Approaching Neil's desk, she asked, "What are you reading?"

"*Capitalism and Freedom* by Milton Friedman." He smiled.

"I did not know software geeks also read sociology books," she said with a cunning smile, arching a brow.

"Well, our society has now moved to media, which we call social media. Guys like me have to study it." He smiled.

"God, you have answers for every silly question I pose. Now get up, and let's go for a coffee."

He shifted his focus back to his book again, mischievously ignoring Apanna.

"You can tell me what you are doing here at night while I finish the last page. Then we will go for a coffee."

"Well, just to have a coffee, I guess," she said. "With you," she whispered, hoping he did not hear it.

"Let's go." Neil smiled and closed his book.

Apanna was elated.

"A society that puts freedom before equality will get a high degree of both. What do you think?" he asked all of a sudden.

Apanna was not expecting this.

"Well, sounds like a topic to think about when I am bored, but not now." She made a face.

"Are you a Scorpion?"

"Yes."

There was a silence for a few seconds.

"Say something. I am expecting some of your cool theories about Scorpions," she taunted.

"Well, I am trying to bore a Scorpion by not talking to her. So she could think about a society that puts freedom before equality, and if it will get a high degree of both."

She lightly punched his shoulder with a cunning smile on her face.

*

Apanna's memories were interrupted by her father, who now pulled over the car at Parathawalas and asked, "What would you like to have, Appu?"

She did not utter a word. She reclined the seat and continued thinking about that night spent with Neil in the cafeteria, the night that somewhat made her what she was today.

*

"So, how is life without parents being around to lecture you?" asked Neil.

"Like a free bird in the sky, to be honest. I am here not because I wanted to do something in sociology but to escape some regular faces which I have been seeing since I was born."

"Hmm. Well, here is something I found on the internet."

He showed Apanna a picture of herself outside JNU. It was two years old, and he had found it on the internet.

"You have a blog, Apanna, with very good content but very few visitors. You might not have put marketing efforts, I believe, intentionally. You have written articles in foreign magazines, which not many Indians read. This clearly means that you want to speak but don't want to be heard." Neil's voice was strong, but he smiled while he talked.

"Did you stalk me?" asked Apanna, surprised.

"Well, I call it homework." He smiled.

"How did you know these anonymous articles were mine?"

"Well, for common men, let's call it a hack, and for the geeks like me, it's called AI. I have created a browser extension that shows me the most related content on the internet written on the same theme from the same geography, and also with the same regularity. In turn, most of the time, they turn out to be written by the same authors. With Google search, it would never be the case, as they have a different set of filters. Plus, I have gained a taste for your writing, so I can clearly distinguish you from other writers." Neil looked straight into her eyes.

"Wow, you have researched so much about me, and I was not even aware. How could you keep that poker face all along?" It was a mixed feeling of shock and curiosity.

"We have been working together for a month, Apanna. And frankly, I like you." Romantic words from a geeky guy are the most unexpected, yet it is a heart-melting moment for a girl.

"What?" Neil's statement almost killed Apanna. She wanted to kiss him right there, but it was her turn now to make a poker face.

"Umm... Yes, I like you. Do you also...?" Neil's voice was still cute.

"Well, we have been working together for a month, and since you know so much about me, and since we are having a coffee for which I invited you, I believe we can give it a try." Apanna could not hold her poker face for long.

Neil held her hand, and she could feel the warmth it carried and a story tingling inside her, ready to surface, between her and him.

They talked the whole night in the cafeteria. He turned out to be an immensely patient listener. They talked a lot about each other, though mostly Apanna. She shared her highs and lows since her childhood with Neil.

She just opened herself up to Neil that night and got a fresh perspective on her personality. She had been in conflict about her true identity all along. That night, she saw a different picture of herself in Neil's eyes. He just went into the deep echelons of her mind and helped her express her core desires and also showed faith to materialize those desires into actions, without fear of getting judged.

Neil's entry in her life cleared a fog of misunderstandings. She now understood that books were not the reason for her so-called 'revolutionary' or 'weird' thoughts, as they called them. She always tried to keep her views to herself and shared them anonymously on social media. A hard-hit victim of the 'Spiral of Silence' theory, which states that if the victim finds their thoughts to be different from the group, they start hiding them with fear of being mocked or left out.

Six hours' discussion later with Neil, she found a source of light in the darkness of lonely thoughts about her own identity. The result was respect for the person she was now in love with.

That night unfolded some revelations about Neil and his ambitions, too. Neil told her that he had been working late nights on a project, which might evade the whimsical forces shaping the world. It was about an internet engine showing the other side of everything we see. He believed that everything is driven by the central idea of consumerism.

"Everything, including the decisions made, sins done, good and bad work, are, in some way or the other, a by-product of consumerism." Neil was confident.

"You mean our meeting is because of consumerism?" Apanna asked playfully.

"Well, the human mind has been evolving to strive for more. You and I are also not untouched. Yes, we both want more love and affection, nature wants more children, probably that's why we are here, loving each other." Neil exhaled a heavy breath while keeping a hand on Apanna's shoulder.

Neil's was not the 'prince charming' kind of love. It definitely was not a fairy tale either, where he would lift her up with his strong muscles and take her into his castle. He was actually the one with whom she could evolve to fulfil her purpose in life, living her true identity. The picture of herself that she had seen in Neil's eyes was more beautiful than the one she saw on her cell phone every day. What kind of love was it where you saw that person in your identity and was always within you? She had never heard or read about such love.

*

How could Neil be gone?

Apanna reached home from the PM's office, and her mind was still in denial. Apanna's mother asked her what she would like to eat, but she was in no mood to have lunch. She took a glass of juice and fell asleep as soon as she lay down on the bed. It was Apanna's way of dealing with depression; sleeping over her problems gave her peace.

All of a sudden, she saw three shadows on the window, one shadow getting bigger and bigger until it occupied the whole room. She screamed and realized she was dreaming.

Neil's departure was too sudden for her mind to absorb. Neil was not just a part of her love life, but a sharpener, through whom she refined herself. He occupied her thoughts throughout the day. The memories of those 45 days spent in the US with Neil started playing in her mind again.

*

Those 45 days in the US were like a poem to her. A nursery poem that you can never forget. All the loving memories of Neil kept on flashing one by one. He used to spend most of his time in the lab, working on his dream project. Apanna, after finishing her work, used to sit by Neil and help him.

He sought Apanna's views on social and political topics as she was a sociology and journalism student. Apanna had a clue that she might be the stick of emotions that Neil might need while embarking on the ladder of ambition for support. But Neil was too strong to be affected by such weaknesses, she believed. Food, or rather say hunger, was the only weakness Neil had. He could never work with a hungry stomach. She used to enjoy watching him attack food like a kid. He would brandish his chopsticks like a sword and pretend to be a soldier. Once the food was finished, he would say, "See, Apanna, I killed the whole army. I am a one-man army."

She clearly remembered the day they had their first kiss.

"What are you doing tonight, Apanna?" Neil asked during lunch.

"Isn't it the labs as usual?"

"I want to take you somewhere. Would you follow me blindly?"

Apanna looked up into his eyes. "Sure, we can go. After all, you are the only company I have got here," she mocked mischievously.

The night was a little cloudy on the hilltop Neil took Apanna to. He arranged burritos, coffee, and mats on a neat place. The silence persisted for an hour while they enjoyed the cool breeze and the smell of moist soil. Lying on their mat and sharing the food, they held hands.

"What do you like about me?" Apanna turned towards Neil and brought her face over his. Her hair spread all over his face.

"Your face." He laughed.

"What about my hair, my eyes, my belly, voice, and these?" Apanna came closer to him and put his hands on her breasts.

Neil could see clearly into Apanna's shiny eyes. He moved his hands from the top of her torso to her belly. They were close enough that she could smell his perfume. Neil placed a soft kiss on her lips. She felt Neil's fingers on her back and then on her neck. Gravity seemed to stop working for her as she was flying in the sky. To her, Neil felt like a mountain covering the land beneath; his grip was tight.

The next two hours were the best two centuries she had lived in her twenty years.

While Apanna wanted to spend the following day with Neil in her apartment, talking and talking. But Neil had already committed the day for an appointment with Prof. Anantham with regard to his project. His project was taking baby steps, which required a team and funds.

Both reached the lab at their usual time.

"Team, I understand, but why funds?" asked Apanna while Neil was giving a final touch to his presentation.

"Apanna, the engine needs data. I need to buy some storage space."

"Dude, how do you plan to get it funded? Do you think big

corporations are going to support it?”

“Well, what justice would a lion bring to a deer? I will not approach corporations,” Neil said, exasperated.

“That’s why you are heading to the Professor for both team and funds?”

“Yeah, Apanna, I am going to present to Prof. Anantham. I have known him since we were at BITS. He has got hundreds of projects under him, and I have my hopes pinned on him. I am well assured of him not making any bones out of it.”

“Ahan... What kind of a person is he?”

“He is a kind and reasonable guy with his roots in a middle-class Tamilian family. Everybody knows about it,” he said, and left to meet him.

The whole day she kept on thinking about Neil and the last night. When he finally came to the lab, Apanna rushed towards him and hugged him. She even forgot to ask how his interaction with Prof. Anantham was.

When she did not receive the same warmth back, she tried reading his eyes. Neil looked a little disappointed. Apanna raised her brows, questioning the reaction.

He sat on his chair and said, “A pendulum needs a pivot, and that pivot has to have a solid root.”

“Hain?” Apanna gave an innocent look.

“This is what Prof. Anantham told me, Apanna. He refused to fund my project. And at MIT, if Prof. Anantham does not fund a project, you better discard it, as there are very few chances someone else is going to look into it.” Neil’s voice was surprisingly angry.

“You are disappointed? You said that the chances are not great, but still, it shocks me that the idea of a revolutionary engine did not move a professor like him.”

"I think he deliberately does not want to fund the project. This is not the Prof. Anantham I have known since college. I told him that I have made a search engine that would gather choices people make as consumers and reveal the bitter truth. Then he asked me why people would allow the engine to capture their private information. I told him that the engine will be based on blockchain technology. Everybody will be contributing to the information, and we will be doing data analytics and presenting it with relevant information. He asked me about advertisements and promotions. But you know that the engine would not force an idea or product or thought, so advertising is anyway out of the question. I told him that for now, we would rely on funding, but later on, we will charge people a subscription fee to use the engine.

Then he asked me to show him the engine homepage. He saw it for five minutes and looked at me. He told me that he was not going to fund my project. I was stunned. All my past 30 minutes' efforts to convince him went in vain. I asked him for a specific reason, and he said that a pendulum needs a pivot, and that pivot has to have a solid root. He asked me to see the updated comments on the university Ph.D. portal and then left the meeting room." Neil finished, reclined the chair, and closed his eyes.

Apanna parked the topic for later and went to finish her day's work.

In the evening, Prof. Anantham's comments on the portal surprised Neil. He called the idea 'anti-social and devastating' in the long run. Neil knew that his engine would be fatal to the current system, but how was it anti-social?

The next day, Neil went to meet the professor at his place. Apanna clearly remembered the conversation between them as

Neil told her later, word by word.

The professor was having his morning tea and asked Neil to join.

"Sir, the engine is to show people a real picture, where they stand in society, in the economy, and the story behind all the advertising firms. How does it make it an anti-social service?"

"Whatever shatters current society is anti-social, my boy."

"If showing them their real position shatters them, it must be shown then. Militancy is not anti-social; it's just a challenging idea."

"Neil, it would not do more than suffocate them and condemn the current system. It's not a solution; it's a problem explained in detail. Ignorance is bliss. Let it be."

"If the engine is explaining to them the problem, it is not anti-social, rather it is a mirror to society."

Professor Anantham did not speak for a while and stared at the ceiling.

"Neil, had it been a population of a few hundred, we could have discussed things as they are, but it's about seven billion people! You can't show a reality mirror and expect a stable system thereafter. Consumerism, a surrogate freedom, is surviving the world now. Consumerism is the pivot, and there will be pendulum motion around it, without anyone noticing it, and the pivot will not leave its place. It's inevitable."

"And what about what we did in Pilani?"

"Things change, Neil. A person's perceptions and priorities change." Prof. Anantham was indifferent when he said that, and his lack of eye contact proved it.

Neil was surprised. Great minds did not always believe in fundamental changes. He bid adieu to the professor and went straight to his lab.

Apanna was working on her project, as usual. Neil just went to her and hugged her tightly. Apanna could feel a student, who had lost faith in his beloved professor, searching for peace of mind against the voices of his inner rebellion. She wrapped him in her arms while he told her about the conversation, word by word.

Apanna's term in the US was about to end, and the very idea of going back to India in ten days unsettled Apanna. It was not that she had never thought of it before, but now, when she was about to move, she couldn't afford to keep it parked.

Consequences of love are irreversible. First you live them, and then they live in you.

Every night for Apanna was about Neil and memories of the time spent with him.

"Do you think I am a pushover?" This was what she asked Neil during a night out at the lab when he was just staring at her.

"At present, you are, thanks to patriarchy. You don't express yourself. As I suggested, you want to speak, but you don't want to be heard. Society dominates you just like it does 99 percent of people. But you have got such a charismatic style of writing, I must say. Your writing is one of the most beautiful parts of you."

Apanna swelled with pride from that compliment from Neil. Some appreciations are special because of the way they are said, and some are special because of the person who says that.

Neil was not just an intelligent coder and philosopher, but also had the power to touch her soul.

As long as she had known Neil, he was the epitome of freedom. He did what he believed in. Nothing was influential with him. He had an explanation for all his decisions.

There were times when Neil made her feel insecure and teased her that she would miss his company once back to India. He never insisted on having a long-distance relationship, and as for her, she was in no mood to leave a company like Neil's.

She found few chances to insist that Neil come to India and continue his project there. India, being a big consumer market, would make a good starting point. Neil never said no to it but said, "At the right time."

Neil was a gem of a person. He had wonderful observational skills and often left her amused. When she came with her hair untied, when she used a pencil instead of a pen, when she put her hair to the left instead of right, when her nose became red during a bike ride. She wondered how such a chocolate boy turned into a genius programmer with a revolutionary vision.

As Neil introduced her to her true self, sometimes she would think about her past self. She never spoke against her father or mother, though she kept a secret grudge against her mother for being extra cautious about her and randomly preaching to her about a girl's duties. Her mother belonged to Allahabad and was married to her father at the age of 18. She had been doing her undergrad then, and after marriage, she dropped out. She became a full-time wife and mother, and there is no addition to her story. Apanna spent almost her entire childhood and high school years in her mother's company. Her father was not so cautious about her choices. She always waited for him to come home during the night when they would talk about their day.

In India, all consequences of a girl's actions are blamed or credited to her mother, including her birth. And Apanna's mother very well knew it. Her name was given by her Aunt Mary. She did not have any children and loved Apanna as her own. Apanna was also fond of her, as she tolerated her mischievous acts, unlike her mother.

Neil always attributed her suppression to the high level of tolerance God has gifted to all women. "You are misusing the tolerance God has gifted to all women kind. You have written about the pathetic social and economic conditions of Indian women; you have written about their pathetic emotional condition, too, Apanna. Clearly, you know you are not exempt. Why don't you use your tolerance power in a flipside way? Let them be against you, and you use your tolerance for that. Who knows what shape it might take? Nobody knows where a revolution starts."

Once he said, "If given an opportunity, everyone should go on a solo trip with little money. It makes you fight for your survival. There you will understand how 'living' itself is a goal, a beautiful thing to cherish. All other relations, materials, luxuries are secondary there, and you start valuing your life, and for that matter, a life in general."

She went to bed every night, thinking about those days.

One afternoon, she got a message from Neil. "I am at JFK and flying to China. Have a flight in an hour. Hope our paths cross again in life."

She felt like she was back to reality and the dream was over.

So many questions were left unanswered. How could he get away like that? Did he get funding in China? Does she mean nothing to him? Was he another manipulative man she had come across?

She got back to India with all the questions unanswered and tried connecting with Neil on social media, but he was not active on any of them. He had shut down all his social media accounts. Had it been some other guy who left like that, she would have been mad at him and forgotten him out of her own self-respect.

But it was Neil. It was about what he made her believe.

His words, his perception, and his view were in her veins. He exposed her to her real self. From that point onwards, she became Lady Neil, deity of her purpose, and everything came secondary to her identity.

She went on lots of solo trips, like Neil had suggested, to discover her true self. Down the line, she emerged as one of the most outspoken journalists across the globe. She would have never imagined that Neil and her paths would cross once again after two years in the most unimaginable way, and that Neil's project, The Flipside Cult, would become her *Karma-Kshetra.*

The wheel of the country lost its momentum with one of her articles, which brought Neil's project to mass attention in India: **"The Flipside Cult: Our War Against Ourselves."** The article very close to her heart.

2

A Peek into Flipside

The Flipside Cult: Our War Against Ourselves

– Apanna Popat

Be the change you want to see in the world.

– MK Gandhi

Ram Sahay Sansi, a native resident of a remote village, *Sansiyo-ki-dhani*, in Udaipur district of Rajasthan, might not have come across the above-mentioned quote by Gandhiji, but has fairly lived up to that. Recently, he got fame on Instagram for speaking audaciously about the transformation he has brought to his village after visiting 'The Flipside Cult', an internet-based tool. I packed my bag and departed to see what all was there to unfold.

"Almost every child of my age dreamed just to qualify the upper primary school and learn how to read and write and do basic math. After that, they join their family for farming. I, too, did the same," said Ramsahay, when asked about his background.

"The village belongs to the Sansi tribe. Almost all of the thousand families living in the village are Sansi. Since independence, the land near the village was granted to them for farming. They had been farming their lands and keeping cattle, until five years back when the factory mafia arrived. With no industry nearby, water levels were good and the crop always did well," he continued.

"We used to wake up early morning, milk the cows, and go farming. Since we never faced a crisis of monsoon and water levels were good, we developed a culture of happy living. No debts, no luxury. It was a village close to nature," said Sansi in his interview.

It would need a hundred pages if I put down everything here that I got to hear from him in an interview that lasted almost half a day. The brief story in his own words goes like this:

*

My village came en route the six-lane highway roads between Delhi and Mumbai (modified from the older two-lane road). With better connectivity, one hundred kilometers away, Udaipur came hours closer to our village. People started visiting the city, especially the young folks. Industries started to shift towards the village as the Supreme Court ordered not to build any industry within a ten-kilometer radius of the city. It was good for industries to find places like *Sansiyo-ki-dhani* as they have excellent road connectivity, water levels are good, and they don't have to worry about the accommodation of workers as people already have their native '*jhopadas*', as one of the officials once pronounced our houses. Factories started employing local people. Every family split the work between men and women. Women farmed and men went to the factories. With industries came mobile towers and DTH antennas, and people started buying channel subscriptions. We also started appreciating the 9–5 work culture as the city does. It gave us leisure time, when we could sit with our family and watch daily soaps. The aggregate income became marginally higher than what the initial village economy provided. Now, farm production was less, but we ended up with the same income and some leisure too. We had no complaints with our lives. We started sending our children to schools in nearby towns, thanks to connected roads. The thing I liked the most about this change was the mobile phone and the internet. I watched movies and read about Bollywood actors. A happy and prosperous life it was. I was 15 years old then, and I spent five years after that serving the factory mafias, until one day, we had a session by the local Panchayat along with the factory owners. They proposed to take our land on lease and start producing. The entire farm production, anyway, went to the factory owners, so it made sense to all the elderly folks. Everybody agreed in unison, and legal work was to be done on the 25th of that month, 21 days away. I was able to see what nobody else did. I had seen in Bollywood movies how Jamindars tricked the innocent farmers and made them serve them.

I discussed this with Vikram Sir, the school principal, who was the only graduate in the village. I used to provide milk in the school for mid-day meal, and Vikram Sir would talk to me for some time during the recess. He would say that even though I was not literate, I had the nerve to see things as they are, just like 'The Flipside Cult'. That time, I was not aware of what 'The Flipside Cult' was, but I always took his statement as a compliment. I liked his company. I discussed with him the implications of leasing our lands. It turned out that we would lose economic freedom and become slaves to the factory owners. Out of curiosity, I asked him about The Flipside Cult. He took my mobile and did something.

"What brand of oil do you use, Ram Sahay?"

"Nirmal oil. Everybody uses that."

"Which school do your kids go to?"

"Spring Dale Kids' School."

"Vikram sir asked me a couple of more questions.

"How much did you use to earn and save before?"

I gave him the right number.

"I have made your account on 'The Flipside Cult' and fed basic information like your age, address, what products you use, etc. There are many more things that are not applicable to you at this point in time," Vikram Sir said, while looking at the phone. "Thanks to digitally transformed India, all information is made public on the internet."

He then showed me the mobile, and we spoke for around two hours about what we saw.

'The Flipside Cult' was a search engine, but unlike Google, it had two search bars. Both towards the left side of the screen, one above the other. And towards the right of the search bar, in the middle of the page, there were information fields, where Vikram Sir put all the information he had asked for.

Towards the rightmost part of the page, the search results appeared. It showed two relationships between the two items present in the search bar.

Book relationship – Supposed to show what has been taught to us to be believed by books by the government, a popular belief of how two entities are related.

Flipside relationship – Shows the other side of the coin, which shows how two entities are related around the central idea of consumerism that suggests how one entity is always a consumer to the other, i.e., there is never a win-win; one has to pay for the other's consumer goals.

For me, both relationships were shown as below:

Book relationship – 'I work for the factory, and it pays me.'

Flipside relationship – 'I work for the factory, and the net pay from the factory is negative, i.e., I end up paying the factory.'

I almost laughed. How could I be paying the factory? But then Vikram Sir showed the analysis towards the right, i.e., how much the factory was giving me vs how much I was giving to the factory.

He explained that the products I was using as a household were mostly coming from urban areas, thanks to the roads' connectivity and local TV advertisements. Turned out that the distributors for the products were the same people who were running the factories. They were the same bunch of people who owned private English medium schools, in which we were always encouraged to admit our children. On one hand, factories transformed our labour from farmers to factory workers, paid better wages; on the other hand, they were collecting back the money through other means. The whole factory setup was just a light show to blind our eyes!

I was surprised. How can an automated engine show all this information? Vikram Sir explained to me that this engine has been gaining traction on many intellectual platforms, and he himself believed in its ideology. The conclusion also made sense to me. Our so-called progress was a regress in disguise. In the name of progress, we were supporting the centralization of wealth, and all we were doing was being thankful to those factories for giving us a better lifestyle. But never ever, the idea or question struck any of us that who defined this 'lifestyle'? Us or them? Vikram Sir told me that a better lifestyle is the government's job, not that of private entities, as the ultimate goals of these entities remain in their self-interest. This boggled my mind. I was illiterate, but I understood the power game fairly. Ultimately, what remains important is who has the power and wealth in the end.

I went to my village and asked the elderly to understand this and not to sign on leasing agreement. First, nobody agreed. Then I asked them not to use the urban products recommended to us and see their reaction. To this, the villagers agreed. Sales went down, but the Urbans were cunning. They started a subscription model. For the ones who were subscribed to these products, the bill would be deducted from their monthly salary, and a discount of 10 percent would also be given. The offer was alluring. I made it clear to everyone that this was another trap. I went to the Sarpanch the next day and told him that I would not be giving my land on lease. I was fired from work the very day, and this was the proof. I went to each and every one's doorstep and made them understand that they were being forced to sign the leasing agreement. Can someone force me to lease my motherland if I am not in desperate need of money? These are the same *firangis* who ruled us years ago. Somebody suggested to counsel a lawyer before signing, to which all agreed.

I collected my trustworthy friends and went to the city the next day. I brought with me a lawyer who made it clear to everyone what it meant to lease land to someone. It was a contract for 50 years. Almost three generations. By that time, factories would have already made them and their generation slave of their so-called lifestyle. People took him seriously and did not sign the document. It was all about information. They lured poor people by blocking information, which put them on the winning side. The information has always been controlled by those big capitalists. 'The Flipside Cult' showed that. After that, there was no looking back for me. I collected some young people from the village and started focusing on our land. We boycotted the factories and put all our energy into farming. Things were not the same as they were five years ago. We got far better prices than what the factory paid us. We requested the government to open schools in the village. Now, none of us work in the factories as labourers, and we are the owners of what we produce.

*

This was Ram Sahay, not even matriculated. The real picture of a village economy moved him so much that he took the plunge and changed it.

'The Flipside Cult', as it has already caught the attention of many global think tanks, has more sides to unfold. Ram Sahay's analysis is just a small part. The engine gives many more details. I examined the situation of a white-collar employee in each of India's top 10 blue-chip companies.

The situation on economic terms was more or less similar to what Ram Sahay mentioned. In some cases, the profit made per employee was a thousand times more than the salary paid per employee. When I interviewed some employees, almost every one of them knew that their company made a lot more from them compared to what they were paid. It did not surprise anyone. What was surprising, though, was that they were not able to save money, in spite of above above-average salary. They accounted it to a better lifestyle, though the real picture is completely different. The lifestyle they referred to was the leisure activities they opted for after a week of hard work and the over-expensive apartments they lived in. It was their hard-earned money, which they rightfully spent on malls, amusement parks, recreational activities, and this is what most of them meant by lifestyle. And the surprising part is, the big amusement parks and other capital-intensive leisure/recreation activities are also owned by the same investors, who have major investments in the firms recruiting in that particular city. They did not take into consideration the air they were breathing, the water they were drinking, and the radiation they were exposed to; aren't they also an important part of lifestyle? Ironically, environment-wise, they are living a worse lifestyle than a tier-three city person.

'The Flipside Cult' unfolded it all. Village or city, the story remains the same. The entity, which lures you with a better lifestyle and pay, robs your pocket one way or another. Ultimately, it's the yearly balance sheet of the investor that shows who is accumulating the real wealth; everything else is an illusion.

Following is the link to the analysis of the top 10 firms and the real picture.

Write your doubts or suggestions to Apannapopat@flipsidecult.com.

*

Apanna did not step out of her room for another week. Meanwhile, she received a notice from the court for six cases that had been filed against The Flipside Cult, some by corporate sharks and some through PIL. This added to her worry. Neither Arjun nor Veera, the other two contenders in the quest, were reachable. Neil's body was yet to come to India. She kept thinking about what might have happened a week ago, so she could connect the dots.

*

The night she got arrested, there was a call with Arjun and Veera, which Neil missed. Just the day before, she had arrived from a no-phone solo trip to Bhutan. She was utterly excited as she got the news of her article about The Flipside Cult going viral. She had just come around two in the morning and went to bed. Around four, her phone rang. It was Arjun.

"Dude, where have you been for the last couple of days? I called twice every hour, just to hear back from you. Everyone is so worried."

"Arjun, this was not my first time. I have been on no-phone trips before. I reached at two in the morning."

"This time, it was different, Apanna. Open your Twitter and see what you have done, girl."

Apanna immediately cut the call in excitement and checked her phone. Her article '*The Flipside Cult: Our War Against Ourselves*' was going viral. Almost 5M likes and 100k shares on Facebook. Facebook, Twitter, Instagram, Telegram—the article was trending everywhere.

She had done things to bag herself a 'Forbes 30 Under 30' award, be it the rescue of children from a human trafficking gang in Assam, exposing a politician in a horse trading scam, or voicing up for the people of a small village for the lack of drinking water. Nevertheless, this was something unbelievable to her. This time it was for The Flipside Cult, her very own Neil's dream project, which could possibly stop the wheel of the world.

She quickly checked the engine's analytics. Searches had increased exponentially, and so had data on the server. The more users, the more data. The more data, the more accurate the engine. That's what they all wanted.

She opened her Facebook page, and The Flipside Cult seemed to be the only topic on her feed. Hundreds of memes were flowing on the internet about what people found on the search engine. This is what made The Flipside Cult very interesting. People could search for anything for which they want a flipside relationship with something, and it would predict. Scalability and scope made this engine very popular in a very short period of time. This was the moment they had all been waiting for. Was it the inspiring story of illiterate Ram Sahay or the brilliance of Neil's engine?

After writing the article, she had set out for a solo trip to Bhutan. She did not know that when she would get back from the trip, she would get this much attention and impact with one single article.

She opened her mailbox to find thousands of emails. Mostly strangers sharing their experiences and having doubts about those. She filtered for the earliest email.

"I am a government servant, and I hold an Economics degree. Contributing to private sector giants to build their wealth was the last thing I would have done as a government employee; after all, I joined government service to serve the nation, not the capitalists. But I was shocked to find the vicious circle of financial exchanges on The Flipside Cult engine. It worked the following way: Big private firms and their employees pay taxes to the government, the government gets rich, and we are paid more. With greater pay comes greater life expectations, and with that comes the giant investors into the picture. I have been paying home loan for 15 years, and frankly, in spite of incremental pay, I am not able to live my life as well as my father did, who had a comparatively lower pay."

The next email was from a PhD student from AMU.

"I always believed that advertisements are not just for mar-keting or to boost sales. This is also about setting a good image in public and keeping them far away from the other side of the business—'the production.' I saw my relationship with a local coffee manufacturing firm. We get cheap coffee here, but we ignore the fact that it has harmed our environment a lot. I found out that the firm had cut down the nearby forest area to grow a coffee plantation 50 years ago. Now, the town not only suffers from increased temperature, but people are also often attacked by jungle beasts, though their number has drastically dropped. The Flipside Cult shows all this data instantly, which a human would take days or months to collect and analyse."

Apanna kept on reading the emails, and the more she read about people experiencing The Flipside Cult, the more she became sure that this young mind was going to change the world wisely. She knew that it would evolve more as more people started using it. Since its inception, it was the first time she had witnessed these many visits in such a short span of time.

Apanna logged out of The Flipside Cult and called Arjun back.

"I am still shocked you arrived safely from the airport. Since the day your article started gaining momentum and impact it started to make, the police have been to all the places where you spend your time. I was thinking that as soon as you stepped out of the airport, you would be caught, but I guess the late-night arrival somehow saved you. The police even investigated me and the entire 'Hind News' crew," said Arjun, laughing.

"Well! But on what charges would they arrest me? My article going viral is not a crime, nor did I present wrong facts." Apanna's answer was candid.

"Apanna, the engine's analysis is based on the information available on the internet. The stock prices of those top 10 firms that you mentioned in the article have gone down, and most of the digital content helping the engine to arrive at its conclusions has been removed from the internet. You have been charged with the provocation of the masses with fake data to shatter the economy."

"What about the articles and data which belonged to 'Hind News'?"

"Those, too. And Hind News too has filed a case against you for misusing your daily articles to advertise your 'product' without getting the editorial board's permission, breaking the conditions mentioned in your bond with the newspaper."

Hind News Agency, with which she had been working for the past two years, was not supporting her; it did not surprise her. Almost every entity has capitalist support as its pivot, as Prof. Anantham had once said. But she also believed in evolution, even if slow. And evolution is a necessity for survival.

"I am happy, Apanna, that this is working now. By the way, I have a surprise for you. We will be connecting over a video call tonight. Neil will also be there. See you in the evening." Arjun bid a warm goodbye, inviting her to the celebratory call scheduled in the evening.

They started the call in the evening. It was Arjun dialling from the US.

"Apanna! Finally, Neil's engine has made a blast in India." Arjun was straight to the point.

"We started big with the place I suggested, our country, India." Apanna's eyes were looking for Neil when she said that.

"Where is Neil? Have not spoken with him since last week because of my solo trip to Bhutan. Is Veera also not there with you?" she asked.

"He went for his music classes for children in an NGO and should be back in some time." Veera waved from behind. There was a sensible mismatch between Veera's words and her expressions.

"Is everything alright, Arjun?" Apanna expressed her concern.

"The engine has become popular there, Apanna. There are people out there who are voluntarily pushing right and relevant data into the system. Now it's not just us four but everyone out there, who is still too young to settle in the crappy system and wants to evolve. No specific age groups," Arjun replied.

"Okay, what now? Iron is hot. Let's not waste the opportunity." Apanna was in no mood to relax.

"Well, it's a friend calling. Let's catch up after a few hours. Will reach out to you." Arjun cut the phone without even looking at Apanna.

Apanna knew something was not right there. But she did not want to imagine what the time was going to unfold. For now, she was happy for the engine and in the mood to celebrate.

Apanna drank, danced, and sang that night, a kind of extension to her solo trip. She called her father and explained to him why she is proud of him! It was her ecstasy coming out as madness; clearly, the joy was too big to hold in the small space of her brain!

It was later in the night, a few hours after she found herself at her home, that she heard a knock on the door and found a police gypsy.

*

There was no hint about what might have happened to Neil that Apanna could gather from the flashbacks, and the worst part was that she was not able to make contact with Arjun or Veera either.

Her excitement of success met a very unfortunate end, and now she just wanted to escape from those flashbacks, but she was not able to. Neil's memories had handcuffed her mind and soul, never to be freed.

Her mind transported her to Congo solo trip where she accidentally met Neil after two years since their time in the US. *What a destiny!* she thought.

She found him leaner and with shorter hair, but she still could not avoid the charismatic gaze that he was the master of.

"A girl who travels solo to Congo, it must not be her first solo," Neil exclaimed.

"Yes, it's not! Neil. How have you been?" said Apanna with her arms folded around Neil's neck and her chin resting on his shoulder.

"Discovering, Apanna, just discovering. By the way, I read about you, and I am happy that you are letting your true self come out. Ms. Forbes 30 Under 30 Journalist."

"Hmm... You always do your homework, don't you?" Apanna laughed at first, but suddenly she slapped Neil.

"Why did you not call me?"

"Will tell you everything, Apanna."

They spent the whole day together in a small forest park by the hillside.

"So, I did ruin your solo plan this time, didn't I?" joked Neil.

"So did I," Apanna replied.

"You know what, Neil, it is always about someone. Your own intuition is a reflection of someone else's voice, whom you love. When you follow that intuition, you reach that person one way or the other. You suggested I take regular solo trips, and here I found you on this most unexpected one."

"Well, Apanna, I know I disappeared, leaving just a message, but it was necessary."

"Good, continue..." She held his hand and put her head on

his folded legs.

"I heard from Arjun after two years since his mysterious escape in the final year of our B.E. We studied at BITS together, and he was my roommate there for two years. He disappeared in the final year and was designated 'Rancho'. The day before your last day in the US, I got a call from him. He asked me to come to Shenzhen and work on my project, which he would fund. But he needed me there as soon as possible. He was having some kind of trouble. I tried to call him back, but he did not answer. I was clueless. It was Arjun, more than a brother to me. I did not have any other option, and if he was in some trouble, I had to go."

"And why did you deactivate all your social media accounts?"

"Well, it is also related to Arjun. Do you believe in hell on earth?"

"Very much."

*

Well, initially in China, it was that. I reached the address Arjun gave me. As soon as I entered the house, someone kicked and pinned me to the ground. I was sure someone was either playing a prank on me or I was going to be kidnapped. I saw nine men, all bald and wearing a 'choga' of pink colour. They looked like some Tibetan monks. I saw Arjun coming from upstairs. All nine people bowed to him.

"Dude, where have you been, and why are these goons bowing? Are you running a gang here?" I stood up.

He wished me and asked me to give him my phone. He deactivated all my social media accounts and deleted all numbers except for my parents. I was sure he had gone mad. But it was Arjun, and he has always been like that, responding to his intuitive calls, without thinking much. He asked me to get accustomed to the house rules there, and he promised to explain everything to me later.

Well, I accepted that hell. I trusted him. Circumstances can change a person's behaviour, but he remains the same inside. It was a part of a cult Arjun had been following—the Karma Cult—for the past six months in Shenzhen, and his lifestyle remained centred on it. Started by an IIT Kanpur '00 student, Cult, or rather the idea, inclined towards 'Karma Yoga', attracted many young explorers.

He later explained to me what it was all about.

The Cult focused on shifting one's activities from consumptive to productive. "The activities you are involved in bring the same type of fruits in the end," was the anthem of the Karma Cult. The Cult believed that there are only two types of Karmas—Productive and Consumptive—based on the fruits they bring. If it brings activity, it is productive, and if it brings leisure, it's consumptive. The smallest unit of the Cult was called 'Family'. Each 'Family' comprised 11 random members. The head of the family made sure that members were not too indulgent in 'consumptive' karma and were more into 'productive' karma. Each and every family member should make sure, by whatever means, that 'consumptive' activities remain in check in the house. Since 10 people observed each other for consumptive behaviour, it was caught easily. You spent time in the Cult and developed productive habits, and then you left for the real world again, with the permission of the head of the family. The kick when I entered the house was meant to make me learn that I should have left the materialistic possessions outside.

Arjun told me that he got to know about my project from a mutual friend, who happened to spot Arjun in Shenzhen and met him. Arjun knew that I was missing one dimension in the engine, which he was living. Macro-level consumption tendency is not just because of external forces. It's deeply rooted in our Karmic choices. If we choose not to be involved in consumerism, we can never be forced to. This is the discovery I planted in the engine's algorithm, and the results were miraculous!

I had a great experience there and got an invaluable partner in this journey, Arjun Shastri.

*

Apanna could see that Neil was satisfied to have Arjun working on the engine. Neil never told any stories about his life, but this time he did, and he conveyed not just the words but feelings.

"You guys are working out of China now?" asked Apanna.

"No, we left for the US and stayed at his uncle's place. After incorporating this feature, we launched the engine."

"And how did you launch it?"

"Well, the way it was meant to be. Initially, I thought of the engine as a means to social revolution and contacted many well-known professors to let me work as a fellow and grant me a team to work with on that project. Days passed, and there was no sign of support from anywhere. Prof. Anantham was not an exception.

I used to work with an NGO called 'I Wish'. While working there, I met its wonderful in-charge Veera. Veera and I happened to share the same alma mater— BITS. She was two years junior to me. She was pursuing her Master's from MIT. She told me that she heard about my project from Prof. Anantham and was very inspired. She is one of her kind. She looks very calm and silent, like a passive bystander, but her observation power is impressive, and her working style and networking skills are awesome. She came up with a brilliant idea to develop and launch the engine. She suggested that the engine is destined to ramp up as an intellectual revolution rather than a social revolution. Ones who are already tagged as intellectuals—the professors—do not want it. We need the hungry folks who strive to fill their stomachs, search for food and an opportunity to prove themselves.

There at 'I Wish', people came for volunteering, and they were some of the brilliant minds at MIT. Law, coding, psychology, you name it, and at MIT, we had brilliant students in each stream. We launched a volunteer project for the engine. It was all within legal boundaries, since the engine is not a profit-making entity, but a service to society. It worked. People volunteered, and we named the project 'The Flipside Cult'. It gave a true sense of relevance as well as belonging to the volunteers, after all, they worked for their satisfaction. Later, Veera joined us in this venture full-time."

Apanna was overwhelmed hearing all this. The past two years had not been rewarding to her alone. Neil was truly living his dream. He had made astounding progress on the engine along with Arjun and Veera.

"This is surprising, Neil. You did not call me even once after coming to the US. You got two more partners and never thought of me as potential help?" Apanna questioned.

"Well, I read about you. You were doing well. I did not want you to leave all of it and work on the engine. I did think of calling you several times. But you know how it has been for me."

"Continue, man, where are you now?"

"We have substantial popularity on public forums like Reddit, Quora, etc. The engine is based on the principle of evolution. The more users we get, the more data to evolve and make predictions, the more relevant it gets, and hence the more users we get. You see how exponential it is."

"Where did you plan to store the data?"

"This is where our philosophy helped. Centralization of power and wealth is what we have been exposing on the engine, and how it is proving to be disastrous in a way. Supporting decentralization of wealth, information, and power to attain a utopian world. So we built the technologies based on computing decentralization principles. It saves and computes on multiple user devices with all security concerns taken care of. Thanks to the expertise Veera brought in with her. Speaking of her, she was the one who recommended bringing the ecology factor into all the features. She is a born environmentalist. She plants a tree every day, you heard it right, every day."

"I am glad, man. We were together when you were working on it, and we will be together now onwards to make the engine work. I am with you." Apanna held Neil's hand.

After the Congo trip, she also became part of the Cult. She actively promoted the engine on her blog and started mention-ing it in Hind News in her articles. The engine started gaining popularity among college students and also on some intellectual online forums.

In a big consumer market like India, the engine got more and relevant data to evolve. Initially, it became famous just because it was serving something new, and people liked spending time on it, sort of a toy to pass their time with. Gradually, over the next two years, people started believing in its credibility because nothing was presented incorrectly. It showed them what was actually happening. The flipside relationship made more sense to people than the blood relationship.

People started giving citations of the engine in their papers, and it became an object of debate as many found it anti-social, as Prof. Anantham had said. Many people tried to anti-market the engine based on its rebellious nature, mocked it, and called it a university project.

Apanna sensed some big hands behind it. She was a well-known face in the Indian media and was on the radar of the white elephants. As they say: first they ignore you, then they laugh at you, then they fight you, and then you win.

Her article proved to be the tipping point for the engine's success in India. This time, it went big, and it was a clear victory for 'The Flipside Cult', which was the brainchild of Neil.

She clearly remembered how Neil's BITSian life paved the way for him to get involved in philanthropy and how his life changed after an incident in his final year at BITS, which made him choose to work for society over an exciting career in corporate. The incident, which could not be more heartbreaking for a 21-year-old college graduate! Neil's story started drumming in her mind louder, after all, his story was the only place where she could see Neil moving, talking, and smiling.

3

Kindness : Dopamine of Superheros

"It's a group of seniors calling us." Neil was woken up by his roommate, Arjun, almost shouting in his ears.

He sat up on his bed and saw Arjun looking at him in panic.

"It is Sai and his friends, planning to rag us in Sai's room," said Arjun.

Arjun's anxious eyes and body language did the trick of making Neil conscious about ragging. The seniors in his Bhawan were all second-year students. It was the day when almost every parent had left the BITS campus, leaving their ward behind in one of the most prestigious engineering colleges in the country.

Let's see whether it feels like hell or heaven, Neil thought.

*

It was an 8x8 single room at the corridor's end of the side wing. Neil realized that it was not Sai, but his room's location in the farthest corner that made everyone choose his room to rag the juniors.

There was a window next to the entrance where he was directed to sit, along with two other guys. He had seen them in

42

the orientation class. Arjun was asked to stand by the gate and make sure that the gate seemed closed, though it was unlatched. Perhaps this was due to the institute's norm that a group of seniors could not be with a group of juniors behind closed doors in the initial days.

In the room, five seniors were seated in a seeming hierarchy. Three were on the bed with their back resting on the wall and legs stretched out. The other two were adjusted between the stretched-out legs. Empty beer bottles beside the bed were testimony to this being a typical engineer's room. The cigarettes among them were like passing on the freedom.

"Grab the chair and sit," one of them ordered Neil.

Neil followed the instructions.

"Tell me, anyone allergic to smoke?"

Everyone shook their head.

"Is this your first session with seniors?"

"No," Arjun tried to bluff them, so that out of pity, they would let them leave.

"Well, then, you are trained. Give us a BITSian salam and also your formal intro," said the guy lying down on the bed.

His bluff backfired. He stared at Neil.

"Well, we met some seniors in our respective cities, but not here," Neil tried to save Arjun. He knew if they got to know that they were being oversmart, they would be ragged harder.

"We will teach you later. First, look at this guy and tell me where he belongs?" One of them pointed at a guy on the bed.

The guy looked like a carry bag. His legs were short, and so was his hair. His complexion was wheatish, and the way he continuously looked at the roof with his hands folded on his belly, Neil was sure he was forced to join the gang to rag them. He was not interested at all. Neil just threw a random guess.

"Maybe Tamil Nadu?" Neil said.

"Because of his complexion? You northerners don't differentiate between South Indian states, do you? A black skinned guy may be from Kerala or Tamil Nadu or Andhra, but for you, they all are Madrasi, right? Then this fat friend of yours should also belong to South India, because of his complexion, shouldn't he?" One senior said while exhaling smoke and passing the round to the next guy.

"You go and come back here in one hour with a list of all South Indian states, their unique language, their unique culture, and demography. And you are going to explain the uniqueness without looking at the list," said the next guy again.

"You, the mother of rats, come and sit!" He pointed to another junior who was sitting by the window.

*

Neil did not want to go to that boring place again. *Seniors are stupid*, he thought. *How can they let him go out of the room while ragging other guys, knowing he could go to the warden?*

He could hear loud roars of laughter from the inside. Either things were not so boring inside, or they were worse for his batchmates.

"Kneel, kneel, you fatso!" he heard someone say.

For sure, it was Arjun's turn now. Neil stepped back and did not go inside the room; rather, he went and removed the fuse of the wing.

Suddenly, the power went out in the room, and someone cried out loud. When the power came back after two minutes, one of the seniors was lying on the ground with a tooth in his hand. Arjun had run away after blowing on the senior's face so hard that his tooth broke out of his mouth. All the freshers had vanished, leaving the seniors in a quandary.

That was the first time seniors learned not to screw with either Neil or Arjun.

*

For a first-year student in college, the whole batch is like a common group. Everybody shares the same courses, and frankly, no one knows what engineering is. When everybody wanted to become a 10 pointer, Neil was playing AOE with other folks he met in ANC—All Night Canteen, every night. Not many first-year students visited the ANC during their initial days, and Neil had already networked with many seniors there. He met seniors working at the Music Club and ELAS, the society that organized English language literary events on campus, and he was recruited to work with them to organize quizzes and other activities. Neil was also a pro guitar player and soon won the heart of the seniors in the music club.

Neil spent his first few months in those club activities, unlike the majority of other students who were burning the midnight oil to be a 10-pointer. After the next three months, the first devil—mid-term examinations arrived. Every fresher was worried about their first mid-semester exams. Even people in the ANC stopped staying for long. Neil was neither in the mood to study nor could he find many people who wanted to play AOE, his favourite game. Being a night owl, he wanted to play but could not find anyone. He found another way to make life more happening on the campus, even more than playing AOE. He created a Facebook page, 'BITS Proposal'.

*

'BITS Proposal' went viral the next morning. It was a Face-book page where the admin selectively showed anonymous proposal texts to a person. Books were stacked on a table, and love was in the air during the mid-term exams. Ninety percent of the proposals were written for girls. The girls for whom the proposals were drafted were either committed or their status was complicated. In the boy's hostel, things were simpler. Wing mates started playing pranks on each other.

Neil pulled a prank on Arjun. He wrote a few proposals for him and posted. He became a hero, but not for long. Ten other proposals were posted for him the next day, to Neil's surprise, and everybody in the wing got an idea that Arjun had been pranked big time! With all the buzz about the 'BITS Proposal', the mid-semester exam time passed.

Then came the music night, every BITSian looked forward to this day. A night with a record number of headbangs and a noise of its kind. Drums and guitars were the most sought-after instruments by the BITSian janta. Some people came drunk or stoned to let their crazy side unfold, some came to enjoy the music, and some came to unwind after the exams.

It started at around eight pm, and Neil appeared on stage around ten pm. Neil's stage appearance was welcomed by a thunder of applause from not just fellow batchmates but also the seniors. Neil was holding his electric guitar.

"Hi, this is Neil. Though I have performed on stage before, this is my first on-stage performance before such a wonderful audience. Presenting to you 'Highway to Hell'."

The connection with the audience was immediate, and it only progressed with his song. All began thumping, clapping, and moving to his grooves. There were hundreds of students dancing, jumping to his song, and this made his fingers go wild on the guitar.

Highway to hell... I am on the highway to hell...

His eyeballs became wide, and his voice became louder. He was lost in the moment, and so was the crowd. He ended with a solo bonus—'Dance of Death'.

Neil was a star now.

In a few days, the mid-semester results were out. Neil topped in four out of seven subjects with 9.8/10 CGPA, very, very high for a guy bunking classes, playing LAN games all night, playing guitar, and conducting quiz sessions. This was Neil, popular among back-benchers and also a curious case for the most studious students, managing academics with extra-curricular, excelling in both.

Two years passed by quickly for Neil. Never limiting himself to any group, Neil was a part of multiple gangs. Two years at BITS had given him a lot, though Neil's favourites were trips to Manali, Badrinath, Shimla, and Dehradun with fellow BITSians and best friend, Arjun. Though he spent time in groups, he was able to truly befriend only Arjun, not because he was his roommate, but because of what he was on the inside. He was one who followed his intuitions without a second thought, always challenging the current stereotypes. He also possessed one more quality, which in medical terms is a disease, but turned out to be a boon for Arjun—He never experienced pain!

Arjun was the student union's president that year, and Neil took advantage of his position for some good reforms on the campus. Neil was active in many student clubs, and he was aware of many areas of improvement on campus. One such area was the MCN scholarship criteria in the college. Students had been misusing it for years, bringing fake income certificates.

He was working closely with the Student Welfare Division (SWD) on this.

"The petition, which you signed with almost 80 percent of the batch, is being reviewed by the administration. Though student testimony is sufficient for that purpose, we might need proof that the income certificates shown by the students, who received the MCN scholarship, did not hold good," said the SWD dean, making eye contact with Neil.

"But would that mean legal actions would be taken for those guilty students?"

"Might be." The warden adjusted his spectacles.

"Sir, with due respect, whatever has been done can't be reversed. We can only change the policy for future batches."

"Neil, look at it this way. People who have suffered are from the student community. People who benefited are also from the student community. Administration is just a provider. And now all you guys have to do is sign a petition and ask the administration to devise a way to provide MCN to eligible students. Neil, this is a premier institute, and we have other routine work. Either give us the proof that MCN provided was not to the right candidates, or we will not be able to do anything." The warden sounded stern.

Neil returned to his room. He did not like what the chief warden had said. MCN should be going to the right candidates. The institute should have made sure of that. But he was not in favour of taking any legal action against those already having them. While battling with such thoughts, he dozed off.

Arjun woke him up in the evening. "Dude, what about the petition?"

Neil briefed Arjun about his meeting with the chief warden.

"Actually, he is right," said Arjun.

"What? Why the hell would you say this, Arjun?"

"Every object outside is an expression of something inside. Moral principles are far more powerful than legal laws. We should explore that path."

Neil got Arjun's point. If students could sign a petition to abolish faulty MCN criteria, they could pledge not to opt for false MCN, too.

Arjun looked at a picture of Vivekananda on the wall.

"You know, Arjun, we need to create a psychological and moral impact. The Internet has made it simpler to do so. A high moral example set might not be able to abolish this faulty process, but it will reduce the cases." Neil was smiling while speaking.

They posted an article on 'BITSians For Each Other', a Facebook page with over 50,000 BITS members, including alumni as well as on-campus students. The article attached the pledge submitted to SWD, signed by ~600 students, to change the current procedure of awarding the MCN scholarship, and the dean's response to it. Without bringing solid proof of past cases of presenting fake income certificates, the institute was not going to change the criteria. The article audaciously requested all alumni who presented the fake certificate and got MCN scholarships to return it back and support the social media campaign the current batch had started for future students, to take a pledge at the time of entrance not to present fake income certificates. The larger the social media campaign, the stronger the impression would be made on future students. Social media is a repository for infinite time anyway. It did not take much time for the BITSian community to understand that some solutions can work outside the system also, based on moral obligations. If the institute was not supportive of bringing any change, students could do it on their own.

The social media got flooded with #MCNForDeservingOnes in a couple of days. Alumni started returning back the scholarship they got with fake income certificates.

Newspapers also covered the campaign, as it was one of its

own kind.

Student union made sure that in the next session the newcomers were told about the internet campaign, its impact, and its importance. The reduced number of fake MCN applications vouched the success of the campaign and also boosted the goodwill of Arjun and Neil.

*

Neil was an active volunteer at Nirmaan, the biggest NGO working in Pilani for the betterment of society.

Starting from traditional volunteering, i.e., free tuition to students in need, public place cleaning, etc., to techno volunteering like high-tech farming, cattle tracking using RFID, pollution control, etc., were available there. Neil's area of volunteering was high-tech farming and music classes. Despite being involved in many other activities, he spared time every day to visit the Nirmaan centre.

"How can you play the strings without looking at them?" asked a 12-year-old, short kid in his first class.

"There is a thousand-hour rule, my friend. When you have done some activity for a thousand hours, you can amaze pretty much anyone with that. That is how you become a master at anything. And, I have been playing since I was 10. An hour a day itself makes 3,675 hours in ten years. You can begin now." He smiled.

"Will you teach us every day, Neil Bhaiya?" asked the short guy.

"Well, yes, you will not be spared a day. If not me, Shweta Didi or Ranjan Bhaiya will come to teach you. Will you come every day?"

"Yes," replied the short guy.

"He will not come, Neil Bhaiya. He is lying," said a girl sitting in the back. "He will come now, but he will not come during crop season, Bhaiya. He will go to farms with his father."

Neil smiled and looked at the boy carefully again. The guy was looking down, perhaps because he was exposed by the girl. Wearing a long-sleeved, blue T-shirt and black half pants. His fist was clenched, and his body language showed a wish to escape at any given opportunity.

"What's your name?" asked Neil.

"Raghav Kumar Jat." The kid looked up finally.

"Raghav, it's alright. Even we don't attend some of these classes." Neil smiled.

*

Neil also used to go to nearby farms to support them with his soil mapping app. The volunteer group built a kit to map the soil's nutritional value. The kit consisted of some soil sensors and a mobile app.

It suggested what mineral the soil lacks and also which fertilizers to use.

It was a Sunday after the mid-semester examinations. Neil visited a farm with his group for soil mapping. It was September, and the weather was pleasant. The unexpected rain yesternight had left its traces in the cool, soothing air. After mapping the soil, Neil felt like staying for some time.

"You guys carry on. I will have to walk back and join you," said Neil to his group.

The countryside is always intriguing, maybe because it makes us feel richer, or the nature fills what is so empty inside all of us today, Neil thought.

Neil was walking on a narrow track for tractors, cycles, and pedestrians. Both sides were surrounded by farmlands. With a cloudy sky at noon, farmers who had sweated for almost 4−5 hours by now, were ready to hog on to lunch. Neil heard the nature whispering and singing in the form of chirping sparrows, pigeons, and parrots. He suddenly wished for the freedom they had, where there were no defined territories for flying. Perhaps that is why the sky became limitless and the Earth always felt small. There were dogs barking at each other.

Maybe humans taught them to fight for their territory, Neil thought. *Thank God humans don't live in sky, or else the innocent birds would also start claiming their territory, and there would be wars in the name of civilization.* Neil almost smiled at this thought.

It was 12:30 PM, and he had been walking for half an hour. Neil tried ignoring the increasing presence of people on the track, mostly on their way to lunch.

A bird caught Neil's attention. It took off from a nearby tree, flew towards the sky, and plummeted down almost in free fall.

What a gutsy bird! Neil thought.

The bird did this again and again, and landed on a farm one time. Neil followed the bird and reached there. He saw Raghav, along with his parents, working there. He stayed away and observed Raghav. The family was cutting the wheat crop; they divided the farm into three areas, and everyone was cutting within their assigned territory. Raghav stole some time in between to watch the sky or play with the squirrels there. They also had a dog there, mostly to protect the farm from *Nilgai.*

He went there. Seeing him, Raghav ran towards him and came close.

"Bhaiya, you are here to have a nature walk, na?" asked Raghav.

"Yes, and how do you know, Raghav?"

"I have seen other students also coming here," said Raghav.

Raghav's mother came to them with something wrapped up in a knotted, clean cloth.

"Bhaiya, you came at the right time. We are going to have lunch. Come join us."

"Raghav, how do you know him? You were never there when he came for soil mapping."

"I told you; he teaches me music in the evening."

"Oh! Bhaiya, you teach *Sangeet* also?" Raghav's father joined them.

Neil greeted him and said yes. They started walking towards a Banyan tree to have lunch.

Raghav took the lead towards the Banyan tree, though everyone knew it except Neil.

"Why do you teach music to the children here?" asked Raghav's father, Tejiram.

"Music is for everyone. These guys are interested in learning. It touches your soul, which is beyond the complexities of rich and poor."

"But we need to feed our body, not soul," the mother, Rameela, interrupted inquisitively.

Neil wanted to reply to her that not all we do is for feeding the body, but he looked at them again. Lean bodies, bathed in sweat. Three wrinkles of anxiety drawn on foreheads. The mother wore a colorful *lugdi* and *pajeb*. She was more talkative than her husband. The old footwear had stitches inside. They kept on walking. Tejiram greeted a few acquaintances on the way.

"The more people you greet, the more will be the visitors, and more money on tobacco and tea," said Rameela.

"Shut up, Rameela! They are '*bhai-bandhavs*'. If not them, who else are we going to greet and meet?"

"But you never visit their houses. The kid does not see anything except the farm and the school."

They reached the Banyan tree and washed their faces and hands with the water they carried in an old oil container from the farm. Rameela opened the knot of the cloth. There was thick chapatti, green chili, garlic chutney, and onion. Two chapattis for each of the parents and one chapatti for Raghav. The parents shared one chapatti with Neil, despite Neil's insistence that he had a heavy breakfast and would be having lunch later.

"Please eat with us, Neil Bhaiya," smiled Raghav.

Neil agreed. They placed chutney on the chapatti itself and a bit of green chili. Onion has always worked like a global complementary dish. They had got a bottle of *chaach* too. Neil had never had this kind of lunch before. It was a magical moment in which he realized that less can also be more and miraculous. He felt that he was sitting in a distant resort in Goa and having thick-crust wheat-grain garlic pizza with extra toppings of onion and green chili, complemented with masala buttermilk. *That's how they sell it*, Neil thought and almost smiled.

Once the lunch was done, the weather increased the need for an afternoon nap under the tree. Raghav asked Rameela to continue the story of Ramayana from where she left the day before. As she was telling the story, Tejiram dozed off. There was a smile on Tejiram's face as he slept. The three lines of tension on the forehead with a smile, Tejiram's sleeping face was a poetic moment for Neil!

Rameela and Raghav were talking like friends, and Raghav laughed aloud when she mentioned how Hanuman Ji burnt the evil Ravana's Lanka.

Is this the same family he was talking to just a while back?

Their clothes were clean, though there were patches of different colours where they had mended the torn parts. Tejiram wore a colourful turban, which he held in his lap while napping. Tejiram's beard was well-trimmed, and Rameela's braid well-maintained. They sent their kid to study and never stopped him from learning music, which, of course, did not make any sense to the poor or the middle class as a career prospect. Neil saw both sides of the farmer family, and he was curious to know more about them.

*

On the way back to their farm, Neil spoke to Tejiram proactively. "How is the crop this time, Tejiram Ji?"

"Crop is good."

"Is soil mapping helping?"

"Your soil mapping helped us to identify the right *khaad*. But this technique brought good results only to those who could afford it. It increased their production."

"You could have told us. We would have done something. Maybe we could help bring some financial support from local authorities."

Tejiram laughed. Neil sensed a strange pessimism there.

"No, seriously, we can help. Even if the local authorities do not help, we can do crowdfunding."

Neil thought Tejiram was going to ask about crowdfunding. He waited for a few seconds, but Tejiram didn't.

"We are the ones who would suffer both at the time of low production and good production. So, our destiny remains the same."

Neil looked at Tejiram, who kept his eyes on the empty road while walking. Raghav and Rameela might have reached the farm already.

"How is good production not good?"

"It is good for consumers because the prices go down with good production. There are indicators if a crop is going to be good or bad. People know it well in advance, except in the case of unexpected weather. If there is an indication of a good crop, prices would be kept low at the *mandi,* and in the other case, we will anyway have less crop to sell, so it does not make much difference to us. Though, good crop seldom brings a financial bonus to us, it does bring satisfaction. Crop is like a girl child. You know it's not going to bring income to your house, but when she calls you with her soft voice, cares about you and runs around, you feel joy inside. It's the satisfaction of creation."

Neil was touched.

They reached the farm. Neil gave a chocolate he had to Raghav and went back but with many questions in his head.

*

The entire week, he worked on an Excel sheet detailing the prices and volume of wheat in the past five years. He gathered the data for different points of sale to understand the overall supply chain. He compared the prices at the first point of sale, the GCI (Grain Corporation of India) warehouses and *Vyapar Mandis.* GCI offered relatively better prices than *Vyapar Mandis* most of the time. He also noticed that, in most of the supply chain, a big margin was eaten by the last point of sale, i.e., the retail market. Farmers more or less got prices close to MSP, decided by the government at GCI, but at *Vyapar Mandis,* it was all market-driven. Tejiram was right to say that even a good crop would not bring a fortune to them because *Vyapar Mandis'* pricing was supply-driven. But why did he not always sell to GCI at MSP?

Neil returned to Tejiram's farm next Sunday at the same time.

They were sitting under the same Banyan tree. Neil brought his guitar this time and gave it to Raghav.

"Dude, come on, play the Vande Matram song."

Raghav was progressing fast in the music class and was able to play the notes and some tunes. He always looked at Neil's guitar, kept in a corner of the room, before Neil entered the class.

He played the song. His parents were happy. Rameela joined Tejiram and Neil for a chat.

"Who do you sell your crop to, Tejiram ji?" asked Neil.

"Not just me but the entire village sells the crop to the *Vyaparis* at the *Mandi* in Jhunjhunu."

"We rent common tractors to send the crops to the *Mandi*," added Rameela.

"*Vyaparis* purchase all the crop?"

"Depends on the production. Sometimes, they buy, and sometimes, they don't."

"If they don't buy, we go to the GCI," added Rameela.

"So, the *Vyaparis* pay you more than the GCI?" Neil asked, looking at Rameela.

"No, never," replied Tejiram.

"We go to the *Vyaparis* first, because they know us. Unlike at GCI, we don't have to wait in lines to get the truck unloaded. The longer we wait, the higher the rent for the truck, and the possibility of theft or the grains getting wet in the rain. The GCI is a government entity. They don't care about us. Officials there get their salary and do their prescribed job."

"Does the GCI buy all the crop?"

"Well, the GCI is where the hell is felt," Rameela answered.

"We don't know when your number is going to come for the transaction, so we unload the truck in the open GCI premises.

There are very limited shelters at GCI for the crop. All the risk is ours only. If it rains and the crop gets spoiled, they won't buy it. In worst cases, we have to sell it to some commission agents, looking for a steal deal around GCI premises at stooping low prices that barely meet the cost of production," she continued.

"Once my crop faced this curse, and after waiting for seven days at GCI, I had to sell it to a commission agent. Three months of hard work, hopes of paying back a debt of 5,000 rupees, and the desire to gift my wife her old earrings, which I put on mortgage, vanished just like that. If something like this happens, you develop a grudge against the crop, which you loved so much. But then all that seems like a bad dream, things go back on track, and we are back to the farms." Tejiram was looking at the sky while talking.

Neil looked at Tejiram. His fists were closed, but the truth was out, loud and naked. Tejiram's story was the story of India. The story of disappointment, fear, and pessimism. Then what about the story being circulated in the media? The story of development, hope, and a shining India?

He left the farm with many questions again, and it felt like he had just left India.

*

Neil discussed this topic with Arjun to get his opinion.

"Dude, it's a dirty game," Neil concluded his story to Arjun.

"How is it a game, that too 'dirty'"? Arjun played his turn in chess.

"The poor farmers produce, but they don't get enough margins on their products. It does not add up any bonus or monetary value, even if the crop does well, as they would still get what has been decided for them." Neil played the knight this time.

"What do you mean by 'decided'? It's a free market, Neil.

They get what we decide. The consumers decide. In the end, the product value is what matters. The whole thing is about supply chain—demand and supply." Arjun took some time to think and played a pawn.

"But what if I say they are not part of the overall supply chain? What if I say that the free market starts from the *Vyapar Mandis* and not from the farmers? And moreover, it's not a completely free economy. The government does have control over some policies." Neil played the knight again.

"You mean the prices that the farmers get are not competitive? They are just getting exploited?" Arjun played the bishop.

"Pretty much. I think so. And not only by the *Mandi Vyaparis* who can afford to store the grain, but the government, too." Neil played the rook.

"The government claims to provide grains to BPL people at discounted prices as per the central government subsidy policy via Fair Price Shops under the Public Distribution System. It has been a big political agenda. It is one reason that BPL families do not blame the government for their pathetic conditions. They compare the subsidized prices with the market price and hail the government for making the grain affordable. The truth is that the government buys the crop from poor farmers, providing them very low profit margins. The benchmark for most of the market prices is also the MSP, which is set by the government, and the MSP is just to provide marginal profits to farmers. Had this all system been designed to uplift the farmers, they would not be living in the same pathetic conditions; the whole system is to keep the poverty and become their messiah," Neil continued.

"You are saying that the hard work of poor farmers is paying for the subsidy the government is providing, and they don't even get credit for that, but the government gets all the appreciation?" Arjun played a pawn.

"Yes. It's not just the taxpayer's money, Arjun, that is making the government rich. Farmers don't pay taxes, but they are getting cheated." Neil did not play but looked into Arjun's eyes this time.

"Is this the game you were talking about?" said Arjun with a brow up.

"Yes, where there is no hero but only villains and victims. Do you really think selling at MSP is a chance situation? It's not. It is very much systematic. For a resource-rich person, it is easy to find alternatives and start afresh. But when you have just a handful of resources, you are the one who is in need. At the GCI and *Mandis*, stories are built to spread fear. Fear of losing everything. I visited the GCI and *Mandis* several times during the last two weeks. Places where you see the poor getting poorer and the rich becoming richer. The government, *Vyaparis*, everybody's interests are bound to each other, and the poor farmers are the only odd ones out." Neil continued the game and played queen this time.

"But Neil, risk has its returns. The *Vyaparis* get higher margins, but there are some times when they face losses too. Farmers don't care about finding the customer and storing the product. There is no strategy involved in what they do. There is no business. They are just labourers." Arjun played the rook.

"Labourers don't own the product, Arjun. There is a difference. They are owners of their land and their products. They are producers and carry a hundred percent stock. This is just a wrong impression we have since ages. Capitalism has focused on outsourcing the work to experts in certain skills, and the supply chain has been made long and complicated because of that. Farmers don't outsource their work. The risk part is where the government should come into the picture. Instead of the *Vyaparis*, who are resourceful and store the grain, the government should provide farmers with cold storage solutions and let them find their own customers, instead of purchasing at MSP. Let the free market start from the farmers themselves. It gives farmers their rightful share and authority over their products, but it would not happen because the government is in no mood to do that. For the government, subsidies must be continued, regardless of what happens to farmers. And check." Neil's rook threatened Arjun's king.

"Hmm... Helping farmers to exercise risk, which in turn will allow them to sell at the right time and prices, consequently increasing the subsidy cost, does not look like a very fascinating option to the government." Arjun tried to save his king by sacrificing a pawn.

"I have plans for at least the farmers of Pilani. Prof. Anantham is going to help me." Neil smiled and took Arjun's king with his knight. The rook had drawn all of Arjun's attention, and he did not notice the knight.

*

Prof. Anantham and Neil shared many common interests. Neil had worked with the him on one of his papers and that nurtured an intellectual bond between them. They could be spotted in the cafeteria and the ANC, and sometimes on the badminton court discussing topics ranging from simple cooking techniques to how Marx was systematically and strategically thrown out of primary textbooks.

When Neil discussed the condition of farmers in Pilani, Prof. Anantham connected it so well with his life. His father, a farmer, worked hard day and night to pay the tuition fee. He had lost his mother to pneumonia after she took a bath in the river at four in the morning for a month to please the god of wealth, Ganesha. His elder sister did not marry but took care of her younger brother.

Prof. Anantham had been at BITS for 10 years as a professor of Computer Science. In Neil's story, he spotted the missing bolt, but fixing it required collaboration between farmers, the student community, and storage owners.

The plan was drafted, discussed with other faculty members, and legal contacts. Everything looked fine. The only thing was to convince the farmers to come and participate. The soil mapping volunteers shared a good rapport with the farmers. They called upon a meeting under the banyan tree, near the Shiva temple on the auspicious day of Dhanteras, two days before Diwali. Twenty farmers joined, along with their families.

Neil and his volunteer group stood on a platform under the banyan tree. A wave of hope and curiosity was running through the crowd. People were chit-chatting with each other, waiting for the group of students to speak out.

"Everything is yours. The '*Agrotpadak—A Kisaan Cooperative*' will be just a common name for all of you," Neil said. "You will not have to worry much about selling your crop at a fair price, waiting in a queue at GCI premises, and suffering a bad deal at last. This cooperative is going to help you find good customers, provide you with storage facilities, and make sure that your grievances are addressed. The student volunteers are going to help you to their best."

"Will I be getting more profit if I deposit my production first in the cooperative account?" someone asked.

"No. It will not be a buy-sell model, unlike GCI, as this is not a trading cooperative. This is a cooperative cell. Once your crop is deposited under the banner of '*Agrotpadak*', you will have a choice to keep it there as long as you want until you decide to sell it to the right customers at a good price. There will be every week's selling price set, based on the current market value of wheat. If you agree to sell at that price, you will get that much amount within the next week.

"What if we get a lower selling price? Who decides the selling price?" asked a young farmer.

"My friend, what we are doing is removing any middleman from *Vyapari Mandi* so you can enter the free market economy. We are also making the selling process easier for you operationally. With these two reforms, you would get direct access to quality customers and get the same prices as in a free market, without the help of any middleman. You will sell at a competitive price only; that's fundamental to this model," answered Neil.

"What about operational expenses?" asked one young farmer.

"The operational expenses include transportation charges and storage rent. With the cooperative, the scale of your business is increased. A cumulative storage and transportation will be arranged. The expenses would be adjusted from the payment that would be made to you for the crop. A bunch of smart professors and students would be handling this, and I assure you it would be at least fifty percent lower than the expenses you bear in the current setting. So more price and fewer expenses."

"But we will have to pay salaries to people running the cooperative?"

"Well, the cooperative will be headed by a professor, currently by Prof. Anantham. The head will always be there to make sure your interests are not compromised. Operations will be taken care of by volunteer students with whom you are already working. They will not take any salary for this work. It would be part of the NGO's social activities."

"Will the cooperative provide a loan? If the prices are not good, and we don't want to sell, we might need money for our household expenses," asked Tejiram.

"Yes. With zero percent interest. The student community here is ready to provide a loan, the amount of which will be based on last year's MSP and your crop in store. You can pay the loan once the crop is sold at better prices."

A loud clap echoed even in the empty fields.

*

It had been eight months since the inception of the cooperative. Summer reached its peak in the month of June in Pilani. Activities calmed down on the campus, and everybody's interest shifted to comprehensive exams.

For Neil, these were the last days he would be spending on campus that year. Next semester, he would go for Practice School 2, a semester-long internship program, and would come back to campus in his last semester.

During his last couple of days, he thought of meeting the farmers registered with the cooperative. He got the list from the cooperative. The number of farmers registered had increased from 10 to 50 in just eight months. As he was scrolling down the list of who deposited their last crop, he did not find a name, which he was sure would be there: Tejiram. *Maybe some error,* he thought and confirmed with the committee. Tejiram had not deposited the crop this time. Neil decided to go and meet Tejiram the next day.

*

The next day, he reached Tejiram's house. To his surprise, there were people gathered, and the police were outside speaking to locals. The family had attempted mass suicide. Poisoned the food, held each other's hands, smiled, and waited for death.

"He had borrowed 50,000 rupees for his daughter's marriage. Feasted the village," said someone in the crowd.

"He was happy with the cooperative and had started earning well. But his last crop was destroyed by *Nilgais*," said someone else.

"Basant's crop also was destroyed. He did not commit suicide," a random voice emerged from the group.

"Basant will eat butter with borrowed money. Teji Bhaisaab was a man of honour. How dare you compare him with Basant?" Someone almost punched the other guy.

Neil rushed to the hospital, where the family was admitted. Currently, the doctor was inspecting the family. He took a seat outside the ward, and looked at the guitar he had brought to gift to Raghav with moist eyes.

"Child is saved." Suddenly, someone cried. "Teji and Rameela died."

Neil ran inside and saw Raghav. He caressed his forehead and kept the guitar by his side. He kept staring at Raghav's unconscious face and suddenly felt like God had put Raghav's destiny in his hands now! A tear dropped from Neil's eyes and fell on Raghav's face, and he slowly opened his eyes.

"Neil Bhaiya, where are we?" Raghav's feeble voice drummed very loudly in Neil's ears.

"Gateway to a new world, dear." Neil wiped his tears and hugged Raghav, never to lose again.

4

Revolution Begins

Apanna's chain of flashbacks was broken by Arjun's text that Neil's funeral would be held in his hometown, Kolkata, at eight the next day.

With a heavy heart, Apanna left the same night and reached the address Arjun had shared. It was a hotel where Arjun and Veera were already waiting for Apanna in the lobby. Apanna jumped towards both of them. They embraced each other with all the warmth of consolation. With tears in their eyes and a smile on their face, they lived and died in that one moment together.

"Did you take Neil to his mom or his dad?" asked Apanna.

"To his dad's house. His mom was there too. He was brought up there."

"You know, Arjun, he never liked his parents living apart. He did not even like his dad that much, nor his mom. He was brought up by his grandmother, and the only time he visited India in the last four years was when she passed away. I met her once, when Neil asked me to visit on her 65th birthday. A kind lady, who left kindness as the only heritage for her grandson and boycotted her own son." Apanna sobbed.

It was four in the morning, and there was still some time in Neil's funeral, so they took seats in the hotel lobby area itself, lost in their own thoughts. All three together would never be that silent, had it not been for Neil's untimely departure, thought Arjun.

"Neil was suffering from leukaemia for two years and was undergoing treatment." Arjun broke the silence, addressing Apanna.

Apanna tried to express her grief with words, but tears rolled down her cheeks, and she almost broke down crying.

"How come I did not have any hint about it? We all lived together." Veera grieved.

"Do you remember his monthly solo trips? Well, those were to the hospital. He did not want any of us to spend time taking care of him. Even I failed to convince him to prioritize his health. But he was different; death inspired him, on the contrary. He started getting more immersed in the engine and used to say that the tasks would be over soon. He used to say that time always comes with a warning, in the form of terms and conditions, but almost all of us never care to read those terms and conditions."

Apanna's eyes began overflowing with tears.

"What about the treatment expenses?" she asked.

"He did part-time music concerts in clubs. Neil's fingers were magic. He did not accept the money I offered, nor did he ask his parents. After his grandmother's demise, he almost stopped speaking to them. Ok, enough. The funeral is at eight. Let's go now," Arjun said.

Apanna remembered Neil's face when they met in Congo. He was lean. But she did not expect him to be suffering from cancer.

He was livelier than life, always. She kept on wondering with teary eyes whether the reason for his liveliness was his life ending, or him wanting to live more.

If you want to know a person, observe the way they live before death, she thought.

Apanna was overwhelmed with mounting respect after un-covering this hidden aspect of Neil, even after his demise. The more she thought about Neil, the more she felt the emptiness that was in the air and inside her.

*

They reached Neil's father's house, where the funeral was held.

Apanna saw Neil's photo in the hall with a garland over it. To her own surprise, she did not feel like crying, but just be there and feel Neil's presence around his body. She saw Neil's parents sitting in the front, looking at his photo. The glass windows towards the left side of the hall were open, and a cool breeze was circulating and providing silence and condolence. The wind carried the aroma of the incense sticks placed in front of Neil's photo. She chose to sit at the back, towards the entrance, and Arjun took his seat to the right of Apanna and Veera to the left. After some rituals, the *pandit* asked everybody to pay tribute to his body with flowers kept nearby.

Apanna saw Neil's face when she went to offer the flowers. Cutting through her temporarily calm mind, that moment became as horrible as she had imagined before reaching there. When she had left the US, she thought it was the worst goodbye and the last meeting they could have. But today, when she saw Neil lying down there, calm forever, she realized that, that was not the worst and also realized that the worst comes along with its silent partner—a will to live no more.

Suddenly, the breeze from the window blew faster and moved Neil's hair, and it set the hair in the same way in which Neil always used to fix them. Was it just air, or was it Neil himself out there in infinity? Her body almost shivered at this thought. She wiped her tears, got up, and got out of the room with a vow to herself—Neil would live forever in The Flipside Cult.

A week after Neil's death, the trio was back in Delhi at Apanna's house. They were sitting by a small wall on the terrace, facing the rising sun, and sipping coffee. In the course of the ten days since 'The Flipside Cult' was banned, they had received summons for six cases filed against the engine.

"Which is the first case?" asked Arjun.

"This case is filed by a government prosecutor, Adil Salem, in the Supreme Court. It says that when he searched the relationship between the Indian Army and the Indian government, the engine suggests a flipside relationship between the two as 'Army is an institution no more bound by constitutional laws, rather used as a puppet by opportunist governments.' This is getting viral and spreading anti-national sentiments across the country," Apanna said.

"Adil Salem, known for his brutal proceedings. Hardly loses any case." Veera added while taking a long sip of coffee.

"How do you know him?" asked Arjun.

"I have read about him in one of the case studies I did in the Humanities course at BITS."

"Let it be. However brutal his story may be, our story is true and powerful," Arjun added.

"What are the other allegations, Apanna?" asked Veera.

"Let me list all of them down:

Engine's flipside relationship of government with army as 'Army is an institution no more bound by constitutional laws, rather used as a puppet by opportunist governments,' is getting viral and spreading an antinational sentiment across the country. A PIL filed by Prosecutor Adil Salem.

Engine's flipside relationship of NHCI (National Highway Corporation India) with select private contractor firms as 'Unfair and much higher ROI on public investments by selected private entities on highway projects' is spreading public distrust for PSUs and trying to eliminate public faith in PSUs, hence promoting the private sector. Filed by NHCI; prosecutor is Adil Salem.

Engine's flipside relationship of the general public and PSU banks as 'Public being looted by PSU Banks, ultimately serving big tycoons with loan defaulting' is again presenting data in a wrong manner to create distrust in public banks, filed by United State Bank of India (USBI); prosecutor is Adil Salem.

Engine's flipside relationship of Brilliance Group with local environment near Krishna-Godavari basin as 'Against it's claim of providing better lifestyle to locals with employment near it's mining facilities, Brilliance Group has made it worse by exploiting the nature nearby and polluting the surroundings' misled the locals workers to go on a strike, and the firm had to temporarily shut down it's facilities there, resulting in a loss of money and its goodwill. Filed by Brilliance Group; lawyer is Shyam Jethramani.

Engine's flipside relationship of GCI (Grain Corporation of India) with government as 'GCI is not a government's instrument to help the farmers, but to appease the poors and keep running the PDS (Public Distribution System) to win the faith of poors in India, ultimately to keep running the political wheel based on poverty' is misleading the public and is full of anti-national motives. Filed by GCI; prosecutor is Adil Salem.

Engine's flipside relationship of news channels with the public as 'Media is a political weapon for brain-washing crores of Indians and manipulating the public sentiments,' is spreading mistrust among people by a skewed image of the media. Filed by Primes Group, lawyer is Shyam Jethramani." Apanna finished reading the notices one by one.

"We have dates for the hearings, and they are not too far," Apanna added with a sip of her coffee.

"Oh! Too soon, isn't it? Shouldn't we be the last one in the queue? There are lakhs of pending cases in the Supreme Court. The engine is already banned. Why would they schedule our case as a priority, as I know nobody would be interested in reviving the engine in India," said Arjun.

"The hurry is not to revive the engine, Dude! It is to fix the public image of the firms, the so-called damage done by engine results," said Veera.

"And they are sure that we would lose the case?" Apanna added.

"Well! Neil, the founder, is not there anymore. In the absence of *Sardar*, the *kabila* falls. I believe they are under such an impression." Veera smiled.

"Hahahaha... if that is the case, they have the wrong impression. This is not a *kabila*. People have chosen us; they have shown faith in the engine. Now this is a virtual democracy, and democracy does not need heir, the only owner is the public there." Arjun smirked.

"I have a few contacts in the lawyer community. Let's get us a lawyer, and let's prepare for the battle." Apanna looked confident.

"Well, I have just one concern. The engine had been banned in India, so no more could be expected out of India. At this point in time, it is important to catalyse a global event that could translate into a substantial faith in the engine globally," said Arjun.

"Where do we start? US?" asked Apanna.

"No, Congo. Neil had been researching the relationship between the people of Congo and the industries there. The mafia has been exploiting the fertile land of Congo with a chemical that destroys forests. He has it all documented. He was just waiting for the right time to go there and expose the mine mafia. I will go there." Veera's eyes clearly spoke of her rage against the mafia.

"Ok, then the strategy is clear. Apanna and I would stay and defend against the cases, and Veera would go to Congo and start a movement for international coverage. This would not only get the world's attention to The Flipside Cult and set its image, but it would be her personal victory too, after all, she is a diehard environmentalist." Arjun felt proud of Veera while stating.

Everybody cheered and gulped the last sip of the coffee.

"To Neil."

*

"Things cannot get any worse." Apanna sat on the couch. "Nobody is willing to take up the case against Adil Salem," she continued.

Arjun looked at the fan for a few seconds and then said, "I will be defending the engine."

"Don't act emotionally, Arjun. The courtroom is not a people's assembly. There are laws, and proceedings are governed by them. We don't want anything to go wrong with the cases," Apanna said in a concerned voice.

"Who knows the engine better than us?" Arjun spoke confidently.

"But rules in law are very complicated, Arjun. They either support the case or go against it, nothing in between. Your knowledge and faith need the wit of a lawyer, too," Apanna said with one brow up.

"We have the truth with us, Apanna. Engine's interpretations are coming true. There are facts to support them," Arjun said.

"Through The Flipside Cult, we are challenging old faiths. The current system is based on old faiths, and mind you, all the economic, social, and political systems are built on old faith. There are going to be very powerful forces to smash the engine, and we need someone as strong to defend us," Apanna almost shouted.

"Heard you. Have you ever heard of a thunderlight triggering a wildfire in just a moment?" Arjun smiled and patted Apanna.

Arjun sounded a little overconfident, but his words always made her feel secure. She always felt that he carried the same 'reality distortion field' that Steve Jobs used to. She slept on Arjun's idea.

*

"Never saw you before, Sir Ji. First time at the court?" the *chaiwala* said to Arjun while he was sipping the tea at the court premises and waiting for Apanna to join. Today was the first hearing.

"Yes. You seem to know a lot about this place. Do you know Adil Salem?"

"Who does not know him, Saab. Six feet, fair-looking guy in his early 40s. Don't judge him based on the fact that he is just a public prosecutor. He is a storyteller, they say. The only lawyer who has defeated Jethramani Sir a couple of times."

"Is it what everybody says, or do you personally know him?"

"He visits my shop for afternoon tea, Saab," said the *chaiwala* while stirring the teapot.

"Do you know anything about Justice Shakti Singh also?"

Apanna appeared from almost nowhere and took a seat near Arjun.

"She is new here and in her late 40s. She is not the daughter of the blind lady, standing right beside her seat. Only some strategic cases are handed over to her. They say that there is no pattern in her judgments. She sometimes gives very unique judgments, which are beyond anyone's imagination, and sometimes she seems like one of those who have bungalows in Kailash. But the only thing that remains common in her hearings is that she likes stories, and whoever tells the best story, wins." The *chaiwala* finished his sentence by pouring more tea into their cups.

*

There were only a bunch of people sitting in the courtroom. Apanna was behind Arjun, and Adil Salem was sitting beside Arjun. Three more people were sitting at the back.

Justice Singh arrived ten minutes after the scheduled time.

"Bring the accused to the witness box."

Apanna went there.

"Mr. Prosecutor, you can start."

"Thank you, My Lord." Adil Salem proceeded to the front. He was wearing yellow-coloured glasses.

"Ms. Apanna Popat, co-founder of The Flipside Cult, why are you wearing a yellow shirt today?"

"It is a white shirt, Sir."

"No, it is yellow."

"It is white, Sir, I guess you need to remove your yellow glasses to see the white color."

"What glasses are you referring to? I am not wearing any glasses." Salem sounded serious.

"What kind of trial is it, Advocate Adil?" interrupted Justice

Singh.

"Apologies, My Lord. Kids need to be taught in kids' language."

"Ms. Popat is representing 'The Flipside Cult', an internet-based tool. After Ms. Popat's viral article, this tool became very popular, and with the support of the innocent public, it became an internet sensation. It did a lot of damage to the government, the economy, industries, and rather to the whole system, by manipulating public beliefs. This is how it works: when searched for two entities, it shows two relationships among them: book relationship and flipside relationship. The book relationship is the one defined by the system. The flipside relationship is something they predict. The engine is designed around the idea of consumerism, and whatever predictions the engine makes are the outcome of an algorithm, which tries to fit the flipside relationship between two entities, centralized around consumerism, as they claim it." Salem passed an official document from the engine's homepage to Justice Singh, explaining the technicalities of the engine.

"Can you please elaborate?" Justice Singh squinted.

"This yellow glass, Your Honor, is the idea of consumerism. These glasses have covered my eyes and are showing me everything in yellow colour. Seeing the world with only one colour leaves me blind to others. Now willingly or unwillingly, I have become the guy with the yellow glasses, or better say, 'filtered truth'. The flipside relationship is this filtered truth, My Lord. While what I see with my naked eyes is what the actual truth is, or as per the engine's terminology, it is the book relationship. Bottom line is—facts are the same, perception is different. The Flipside Cult has presented the facts to people with a different perspective, which in turn is a sociopathic approach, as fundamentally they would always suggest a perspective that would show consumerism in a bad light, which is anti-social, as current society and economy are based on capitalistic values, which rely on consumerism. The court is the keeper of the law and the system, so I request the court to forever ban The Flipside Cult."

"Can you explain the relationships again?" asked Justice Singh.

"Yes, relationships among people, organizations, governments, climate, etc. You can type any two names and see relationships between them."

"Any examples?"

"Example is this case itself, Ma'am. Let me show you a live demo." Adil Salem brought out his mobile phone.

"Since the engine is banned in India, I have connected my phone to the US VPN, and I am able to access the engine. This is the homepage." Salem showed the phone to Justice Singh.

"I typed Government of India in one search bar and Indian Army in another. Now it asks me some more details about these two to find their exact identity and position in the current political, economic, social, and geographical system. There are some known identities, i.e., government, states, registered institutions, for which we get auto-suggestions in the search bar; no need to provide any additional details. But let's say I search for an individual; I might need to provide some details, i.e., my citizenship details, income, address, profession, etc., for the engine to identify me and position me right in the current system. Once this is done, it gives two relationships, i.e., for this instance, the book relationship is that the army is a constitutional body, intended to protect the sovereignty of the Indian democracy. But the flipside relationship says, 'The army is an institution no more bound by constitutional laws, rather used as a puppet by opportunist governments.' This is how the engine concluded it. Maybe Arjun Shastri can take that up." Salem put the phone in his pocket.

"Arjun Shastri, please proceed with the defense." Justice Singh signaled Salem to take his seat.

"Thanks for the lovely story, Advocate Adil." Arjun stood up.

"May I borrow your funny yellow glasses, please?"

"Sure."

"Your honour, the prosecutor was so involved in the story that he forgot to tell an important part of the case. Anyway, I will do it. There are six cases against the engine, and today the hearing is about the first one. Before I proceed to the point, let me finish the story that Advocate Adil started. He called us kids, so yes, we are kids. As kids, we dream and we know very little of worldly affairs; we dream without boundaries.

The engine is compared with yellow glasses. I accept we are putting yellow glasses on people's eyes. But what if the naked eye is not able to see the truth? With naked eyes, right from the beginning, we have been seeing the Sun revolving around the Earth. Does it really mean that the Sun revolves around the Earth? When Copernicus proved this wrong, not many followed his theory, but now everybody knows that the Earth revolves around the Sun, even if every day, they still perceive the Sun revolving around the Earth. There has been a mental filter put for this particular observation to discard the naked-eye observation and to believe the truth. These yellow glasses are that filter, Your Honour. The book relation is the observation that the Sun revolves around the Earth, but the flipside relation here is that the Earth revolves around the Sun, and that is the truth."

"Can you please elaborate on how the engine comes up with the 'flipside relationship'? asked Justice Singh.

"Sure, Ma'am, adding to my friend Adil, let me explain how the engine actually works. From a user's search to the display of the relationship, there are five processes happening in the backend.

The first one is **identity positioning.** The objective of this process is to identify the user searches and put them in the right position in the overall system. We all carry a unique identity as per specific context, i.e., politically, I am a citizen of India; at my home, I am Arjun, the late sleeper; by profession, I am an engineer and an entrepreneur. When we input two entities in the search bar, the engine maps each entity to its unique political, social, and economic identities and finds the right position in its multidimensional identity model."

"Currently, our government IDs are based on a single ID number and single identity. What is a multidimensional identity?" asked Justice Singh.

"Meaning, it accounts for all the identities of the entity, i.e., political, social, economic, etc., and assigns it its own hypothetical unique identity, which has multiple identity variables. It's a virtual model where not only humans, but anything can have a unique identity, i.e., industries have a unique ID, a pubic garden also has a unique identity."

"And how do you assign that identity? How do you know where the entity should lie in the multidimensional model? Do you take some additional user inputs along with the searches?"

"For some well-known entities, we don't need additional user inputs. We just put two entities, and the engine is able to identify those without providing any further information, i.e., governments, big industries, environment, nouns like tree, jungle, lion, etc., but sometimes, it might need some more data for positioning, i.e., some person in Jaipur is searching for his relationship with local government. It might need some more data, like income, age, etc., to assign the right identity to that person.

"Very well."

"After identity positioning, the second process is **data collection.** The objective of this process is to gather relevant data pertaining to those entities for further analysis. The engine uses the search keywords and looks for historical data related to those identities, across the websites on the internet."

"That's very ambiguous, the internet has data in many forms, i.e., web pages, videos, etc. Plus, the internet is an infinite pool of data. Doesn't it take very long to search?"

"Yes, Ma'am. It's unorganized data, as it searches through the internet from blogs, websites, videos, wherever possible. For computing, we have a large number of node pools defined on different hosts, and the search time is very less due to that. The engine has an inbuilt converter that transforms unorganized data into information."

"Marvellous!"

"As an outcome of this step, the engine lists all entities with which either of the searched entities has done any kind of activity in the past, and it also makes a rough model of how all these entities are connected. In this case, when we searched the relationship between the Indian Army and the government, it collected all the data points regarding the entities the army has worked with in the past, i.e., citizens, government, constitution, terrorism, etc., and how it worked with them. Similarly, it gathers data for the government, too. And then it keeps the data where entities are common for both the searched entities. We call these 'simulation entities'. For example, in this case, citizens, politicians, terrorism, militancy, etc., are simulation entities who have worked with both the army and the government."

"So when a user searches two entities, the engine would search for historic events for the individual entity and figure out identities with which those entities have worked with, as you said. Those identities, common to both searched entities, are called simulation entities, which I believe you will be referring to in the further steps."

"Yes, My Lord. This data is fed to the ICT LLM model. The third process is to run the **ICT LLM model**. Integrated Consumerism Theory (ICT) is a paper published by Neil, which has been cited in many other published papers and has earned Neil a Nobel Prize nomination in economics. The theory gives a fresh perspective on consumerism. In a nutshell, the theory states that consumerism is not just an economic term; it is there in every social, economic, or political transaction in the capitalistic era. In every activity of two entities, one entity is the consumer and the other is its provider. The consumer entity will try to gain maximum advantage of the opportunity present, and the provider will always be exploited."

"Isn't it confusing? Consumers are the ones who should blame capitalists for their exploitation. In ICT, consumers are the ones who are exploiting the providers. Can you explain how?"

"Actually, as per ICT, consumers are those who are consuming maximum resources, and providers are the ones who get exploited by those consumers. Consumers in ICT are not the end consumers of goods or services, but the ones who are consuming the maximum benefit of available opportunity."

"Sure, got it, please proceed."

"Thank you. When searched for two entities, one would always be a consumer and the other would be a provider, but which one? To figure out, the ICT LLM model is run. The ICT LLM model is a Large Language Model trained with ICT. It first makes the first searched entity the consumer and the other provider. It then simulates the consumer entity's behaviour with each simulation entity, listed in the last step, one by one. It would record how, as a consumer, the entity behaves with the simulation entity. After that, it makes the other entity a consumer, and repeats the simulation process, keeping the data for the next step, which is testing."

"Hold on. In this step, we are trying to figure out which entity out of the two entities is the consumer, and for that, the engine makes the entity a consumer turn by turn and sees the behaviour of the entity on the simulation entity. So in a nutshell, the engine is just trying to guess what-if scenarios, and in the next step, whatever what-if scenario goes with the testing, that particular guess is approved by the engine, right?"

"Yes, Ma'am, you are right. In layman's terms, it tries to figure out how a consumer entity can exploit the simulation entities to the maximum possible extent, and in that case, how the provider entity will behave. It stores the data for each case for the fourth process, called **boosting.** The objective of boosting is to figure out which of the two entities is more likely to be a consumer. In the previous step, it was all a simulation based on the ICT model. It has data for both saved as the outcome of the last process. In this process, it looks through the historical data to strengthen one of the two hypotheses. One by one, it checks the correlation between the actual historical data collected and the behavior of each entity, in each case.

The positive correlation is an indication of a correct prediction. Meaning, the engine is able to test and check which of the two entities is the consumer and which is the provider and how, with the help of the model and past data available on the internet."

"So is it a black and white picture? What about the degree of consumerism?"

"It is not a black and white picture. The answer is in the last process called **conclusion.** Based on the correlation factor and other variables during testing, the engine is able to decide the degree of consumerism involved between two entities and hence is able to predict the flipside relationship, i.e., how one entity is exploiting another."

Arjun stopped speaking for a glass of water.

"Interesting. It means, irrespective of whatever you search, the engine would show something negative about one identity as per the idea of consumerism," asked Justice Singh.

"That's true, but most of the time they hold good, because it's true. It is a consumerist era. People love the engine because it shows them the flipside, the truth. The document for consumerism theory is on your desk, Ma'am." Arjun was firm.

"Sure, I will look into it, but can you please take the example of this case and explain all the steps?" Justice Singh's voice sounded curious.

"Sure, Justice Singh. The detailed description is in the document provided to the court; I will just try to take one example. Positioning part is not complex here, since both the government and the army hold very strong political identity, in the multidimensional mapping; also, political identity dom-inates for both. In the data collection phase, the engine has looked at post-1947 data, when the government was formed and the army was institutionalized. The Internet was invented much after 1947, but through accredited websites, blogs, and textbooks available on the Internet, it gathered data points for both the government and the army. Be it Naxalite militancy or the Kashmir issue, or the 1971 and 1999 wars, or rescue operations, the engine collected all data points related to the army. Similarly, for the government, right from its constitutional definition to emergency, the careers of political parties, citizens, constitutional amendments, etc., it collected all the data. Then, as explained previously, it found simulation entities, which are common for both, i.e., citizens, militancy, emergency, wars, weapons, etc., and then it applied the ICT LLM model.

In this case, it first took any of the parties to be a consumer. Let's say it made the government a consumer; it would then see how the government can take maximum advantage of simulation entities, i.e., weapons, militancy issues, wars, emergencies, and in those states, how the army would react. It then stored the hypothetical behaviour for testing. Similarly, it made the army a consumer, and it then saw how the government behaves and stores the data for testing. In the testing phase, it checked the correlation between the predicted behaviour and the actual behaviour.

In this case, the prediction of the government being a consumer is right with a strong positive coefficient, and the behaviour of the army was in line with the engine's predictions. The government used all simulation entities to the maximum extent just to win public faith and to come to power again. Be it Naxalites, militancy, emergency, war, or weapons, the government used them, and the army behaved like a puppet to the government, as predicted by the engine. Since the correlation coefficient is good, the conclusion is also very strong." Arjun finished his statement with a strong voice.

"Interesting... We are out of time, so the court is adjourned for today. Next hearing will be next week, same time." Justice Singh called off the session.

*

While having dinner, Apanna and Arjun discussed the next hearing.

"The army has a huge emotional sentiment across the country. The case is creating negative sentiments about the engine, even among the people who initially supported it. People are on the streets to stop the trial and execute all three of us." Apanna was continuously scrolling her phone while holding chopsticks in her hand.

"Not army, Apanna, people's faith is with soldiers. They are their hero. We are not commenting on the soldiers. We are raising concerns over the misuse of the institution named 'Army'. People just need to understand the difference between the two." Arjun finished his manchow soup.

"You are right. And how exactly do we do it?" Apanna asked.

"Vibhishan. We need to find our Vibhishan, who belongs to the *Rakshasas*, but sees the wrongdoing happening there." Arjun smiled.

"And since your 'Vibhishan' will be a soldier, speaking about how the army is being used, people will be listening to him patiently. Excellent." Apanna smiled back.

"Well, I know a Vibhishan, and I'm leaving tonight to bring him. Will see you the day after tomorrow," said Arjun and went inside his room.

And again, Arjun's spontaneity surprised Apanna. In the last hearing, Arjun proved his words. She was now confident that Arjun could defend the engine in all cases. Anyway, she knew

Arjun's true potential. Neil once mentioned his spontaneity and determination in his mail. She opened Neil's earlier mail, where he mentioned Arjun saving the engine from getting banned in the USA.

I can't tell you, Apanna, what Arjun made possible today. He almost saved the engine from getting banned in the USA. A user in Ohio searched for the relationship between a local shoe-making company, 'Lila', and the famous brand, 'Klash'. Surprisingly, the engine came up with a flipside relation that both companies are partner companies and sell similar quality products at different prices. Though, on paper, these companies were not related. Customer reviews matched very closely on top e-commerce sites. The shoe's average life, common problems, everything matched, except one thing—the price. While 'Klash' shoes are priced at $200 average, 'Lila' starts from $30 and goes up to $100. That guy posted the flipside relationship on Twitter and mocked 'Klash'—"Looks like we pay extra $ just for the calligraphic fonts 'KLASH'. The tweet went viral in Ohio. 'KLASH' filed a suit against The Flipside Cult. 'KLASH' is a well-known brand globally. Something was wrong in Ohio. The next day, I woke up and found a note from Arjun—"Going to Ohio, will be back in two days," and he did come back in two days, with a satisfactory smile on his face.

He told me, "Though there is no legal record of partnership between the two firms, they have been doing illegal business in Ohio. There are two assembly lines in the 'Lila' manufacturing plant in Ohio. One is for 'Lila' and another is for 'KLASH'. On record, the output of each assembly line is mentioned as half the real output. For both assembly lines, the suppliers for raw materials are the same, meaning both assembly lines are producing similar quality products. The output of one assembly line is taken to retail showrooms, whereas the output of the other assembly line is loaded into garbage trucks. The interesting part comes now. Nobody doubts the garbage trucks, where they go, or what is inside them. The garbage trucks from the 'Lila' factory go to the 'KLASH' manufacturing plant. It unloads at the 'KLASH' plant and collects garbage from there. Hence, nobody suspects that something is being transacted between the two firms. 'KLASH' manufacturing plant in Ohio does nothing but mark its own brand on 'Lila' shoes. And that's how Ohio rating and quality matches for both the brands."

I asked him how he managed to find all these things in two days.

He said, as always, "I went out of the system to know all this. Ground-level workers, i.e., guards, factory workers, and truck drivers, know the ins and outs of the system, and I targeted them. After that, it was not a big deal to connect the dots and validate the hypothesis."

With photographs and other testimonials from truck drivers, we proved that the companies were involved in illegal activities, and the Ohio plant for 'KLASH' is going to shut down. The engine just tried to predict based on data available on the internet and fit the relationship around consumerism theory, and it was right. We won the case, thanks to my mysterious friend, Arjun.

Arjun had some medically approved superhuman capabilities; she knew. But no superhuman is motivated enough without a story. He, too, had a story that made him choose his bright side over the dark one.

5

Fueling the Fire Within

"Your child, Arjun, is one in a billion, Mr. and Mrs. Shastri." Dr. Naidu entered his cabin and took his seat, speaking to the five-year-old child's parents.

"We didn't get you, Dr. Naidu." Som Shastri looked at his wife, Nita Shastri, and turned back to Dr. Naidu.

"This is a rare medical condition, which occurs with a probability of one in a billion. Let me explain. What would you do when you face a danger?"

"Anything to safeguard my existence," replied Som Shastri.

"Very true. Whatever possible. What would you do if you find out that you feel danger every moment?"

"Well, I will go mad."

"And I believe by madness you mean, you will cry, you will lose your sanity, technically not be able to live in society, am I right?"

"Yes, I guess."

"Mr Shastri, you are a grown-up person. You have seen mad people in life, so you have a definition for 'madness', but what if someone does not know the term 'madness'? You know why we

87

have a pediatrician? Because a child's body and brain cannot be treated like an adult's body and brain. A child's responses will always be different for some medical conditions than adults."

"Yes, we got it. Now, please tell us what Arjun is suffering from."

"It's a condition, not a suffering. Empathy dominates his brain to an extent that he cannot comprehend the difference between different classes of people or animals. For him, every living being's existence is as important as his own. Everybody is blessed with empathy, but for Arjun, empathy surpasses any other emotion, even love, i.e., when he eats food, he will not be able to digest the fact that there are some people living without having a single bite somewhere. For his brain, this will be a sign of danger to humanity, and in turn, to every human and eventually to him."

"But it's a child's mind, and it will learn. Won't he learn gradually that there are different levels of the food chain, different classes among people? You are saying that he will not be able to accept the reality and never learn to live by the political and social laws?"

"No. He will learn everything. He will live a healthy life. He will 'know' the governing forces out there, but he will never be able to digest them. And this indigestion will manifest itself in different forms at different stages based on his capabilities."

"So, he will turn into a monk someday?"

"Quite the contrary of it. He will seem very normal and respond as expected to the world around him. Empathy would work just as a catalyst; the actual chemical reaction will be different. Though his different journey starts with higher doses of empathy, he will taste many other flavors in reaction to his behavior. What he will ultimately become depends on how life unfolds for him. Being a five-year-old, unable to revolt, his mental aggression is getting suppressed and resulting in high blood pressure, headache, and frequent fevers."

"Is there no treatment?" asked Nita Shastri.

"This is not a sickness, Nita, it's a blessing, I feel. Our love and patience will be vital in shaping his personality." Som Shastri held Nita's hand and said goodbye to Dr. Naidu.

*

Though Arjun was good at academics, he kept himself socially distant. For his teachers, it was his nerdy behavior that kept him from socializing with people. But inside, only Arjun knew that he wanted to talk to everyone he met. He wanted to talk for hours, but he could not. He spoke only with his father, with whom he played golf every weekend, and sat on the terrace every day to talk about his day.

Arjun lost his mother at the age of 15 in a road accident. His medical condition started worsening after her death. He used to get frequent headaches, which would last for hours. One night, the pain became insurmountable, and it changed Arjun forever.

"The level of pain was 10 times more than labour pain. The human body is not fully capable of bearing such pain. People die before reaching this far. It has left Arjun with so many irreversible medical conditions. We call it the reversal of survival skills. Pain is necessary to instill the right survival skills in every living being. In the absence of survival skills, he would dare to do things that a normal person can not, i.e., jumping from a building. He would not fear jumping from a building; his bones would break, but he would feel very little pain," Dr. Naidu explained to his father.

"It would be for good or for bad?" asked Som Shastri.

"Depends on Arjun, how he handles it," replied Dr Naidu,

curious himself.

*

Arjun entered the BITS auditorium with Neil after teaching those ragging seniors a lesson. It was a huge, closed auditorium, better known as 'Audi'. As he stepped in, he was asked to show his ID card by a guy labelled as 'Audi Force'. Arjun almost laughed at the name. 'Audi Chowki' would suit him better.

The auditorium was dark inside, with some disco lights hovering over the front seats and the stage lit. The students were making noise, and the music was loud.

Arjun saw Neil already humming the song being played, and his hands in the air followed the music.

"What's this music, man? Never heard of it," asked Arjun.

"Eluveitie Inis Monaaaaaaaaaaaaa. I just love it man, wuhuhu..." Neil shouted loudly.

Arjun, too, became lost in the music after some time. He glanced through the shifting focus, lights emanating from the disco ball above, falling on each head like stars dancing and jumping. Everyone around was of his age. The orientation program was organized by the student union to introduce the BITS student culture to new students. The more Arjun got to know about things to do at BITS, the more energized he felt. He did not know whether it was going to be four years of escape from reality or four years of really knowing himself at BITS. But, at this very rare moment, he just forgot who he was and what he wanted to be, while wishing to live his heart out here.

Arjun went to almost all student clubs and recruitment departments, except for the ones whose time clashed with the ones on his priority list. Finally, Arjun joined the Hindi Drama Club, the Department of Controls, and the Department of Sponsorship. The Department of Sponsorship was recommended to him by his school senior, and he was selected without demonstrating any particular skills, as he was the son of a Jaipur-based business tycoon. Arjun developed a taste for athletic activities too. He would go to Taekwondo classes in the morning, running in the evening, and swimming on the weekends.

Arjun loved spending time in the theater the most. His voice was loud, and his modulation was the finest. He remembered each and every line of the script in just one read and needed the least practice to perform the best among all on stage. The fact that Arjun was so good at acting, saved him from being ragged again by the club's seniors. They loved this guy.

*

Arjun was in charge of execution in the Control Department for Oasis, the five-day annual cultural fest at BITS. Students across the country participated in the fest, and the five days were the most lively days of the year at BITS. MAMO—Mr. and Ms. Oasis event was a special attraction for all, where the participants could show any talent. Arjun also participated in it. He sang a rap song.

"Hit me a stone, or hit me a heart,
Blood in my veins is not gonna stop.
I will still look into your eye,
There will be fear, and red will be sky.
Warm will be blood, out from my veins,
I will burn you along with your dreams,
'Back stabber me' will be written on your face,
Your life will become a disgrace.
Then I will cut your heart into two,
One I will keep and the other will screw.
World will see black blood in that part,

Fair skin out and a demon in heart.
I will then cut my heart into two,
One I will keep and fix other to you.
Red blood will wipe the black blood there,
Pure will be heart, and truth will be bare!"

"Arjun... Arjun... Arjun... Arjun..." Guys cheered for him more than the girls did.

Arjun was overwhelmed.

After his performance, he sat beside Neil and watched the other participants. Suddenly, he heard a loud noise. A girl slapped a guy. The slap was loud enough to divert the attention of the audience.

In the rush of the moment, the guy hit the girl back, and she started crying. As soon as the guy turned around and was about to leave, he faced an intense blow to his face and fell to the ground. Arjun hit him so hard that his nose started bleeding, and he was not able to comprehend what had just happened. Soon, he became unconscious, only to find himself in the hospital the next day.

*

Arjun's father was called to the college. Arjun was already summoned to the dean's office.

"He was a first-year student from Hindu College. I don't know whether students will come to attend Oasis next year. Leave that, that guy is going to take almost six months to recover. His academics are ruined. Do you understand how much pain it is for him?" Dean asked.

Arjun remained silent.

"Outsiders are calling you a rude villager. Did you try to understand what happened before you decided to punch him?" Dean fired another question.

"I did not feel it necessary. The girl who was crying, I knew her. I felt something was wrong. So, I just acted upon my gut feeling, Sir," Arjun answered.

"This is an institute that prepares professionals, Mr. Shastri."

"I was in charge of the Control Department."

"You could deregister him, Arjun. This was supposed to be done professionally. You can go now."

"Mr. Shastri, I know his medical condition. But I have to run a college. Please make him understand and make sure that this is repeated," Dean told Arjun's father.

*

The incident disturbed Neil. Neil had been observing a rise in his dominance and anger with the rising fame. Was it just suppressed childhood deprived of love, or was there more to uncover in this 'pain factor'? As Neil was trying to connect the dots while seated on the wooden chair in his room, Arjun's father entered.

"Hi, Neil, how are you?"

"Hi, Uncle, I am good, how are you?" Neil welcomed him with a pleasant smile.

"How's your Mom and Dad and family?"

"They are good," Neil answered in a low voice.

"Great. I have brought Kishangarh's *Makhan Bada*. Arjun loves them. I guess you have also developed a taste for them, as Arjun told me last time."

"Oh, yes! The most delicious sweet I have ever tasted. Makhan Bada is the king of sweets." Both laughed.

"Arjun won't talk to me, Neil, so give him my wishes and tell him that he is not alone. His father is there with him, always."

Neil was surprised to hear the kind words from Arjun's father after such an incident.

"Listen, Uncle. Do you have some time?"

"Sure, tell me."

"Arjun tells me he has high tolerance to pain, and I have seen it. It unfolds in many forms. But I really don't know whether it is good or bad. Where will it lead, Arjun? He does things in ways no one can. He is called 'Finisher Without Prep', 'Man in Action'. He just sees a problem, comes up with an instant plan, and acts upon it. I really don't think sheer resistance to pain would do such things. Had it been so, animals with high pain tolerance would have taken over the world. Is there something else I need to know?"

Som Shastri sat on the cot, looking at the ground, and explained Arjun's medical condition regarding empathy dominance to Neil. He left after some time.

Neil was thinking about Arjun, how his medical condition had made Arjun reveal himself in different phases of his life. He had been observing aggressive thoughts dominating Arjun for the past couple of months. *Is it how he is going to evolve in his youth?* he thought. *No, I will not let it happen.*

He slept on this thought, rather with determination.

*

Arjun's fame got him presidentship of the Student Union in the third year. One Sunday, Arjun found that there were not enough sweets for the students in the mess.

"Budhiya Ji, there are no sweets today for students?"

"They are finished, Bhaiya Ji."

"But it is always counted and then brought to the mess."

"The vendor brought only this much."

Arjun got out of the mess.

The system is corrupt, he thought. *The local vendors don't have any metric for quality or hygiene, and on top of that, these guys compromise on service, too.* His thoughts almost brought him to the conclusion that the mess was not in the right hands.

Those days, Neil started spending more time on his crop project. He hardly had time to talk for hours like they used to do, and Arjun, too, became very busy with the Student Union-related work and academics.

He called a meeting with the mess representatives in the evening.

"Who is in-charge of procurement for our mess?"

"It's a local vendor. He has been working with us for 20 years."

"So, we send the requirements, and he delivers and gets the payment. That, I believe, is the model, right?"

"No. We give them the number of students for every mess, and they suggest the procurement quantity."

"Do we have a system in place where the quality of raw materials is verified?"

"No. But there are regular checks by the institute."

"What about accounts?"

"Taken care of by the institute."

"Technically, we don't know what the quality of the food is. They are serving on a daily basis, and the supplier has no metrics to ensure the quality of food every day. I have called a global caterer representative tomorrow. They will look at our process and suggest improvements, and if needed, they will get the right to cater food to us. I have spoken to Chief Warden and SWD Dean."

*

When Neil came after attending the tech fest at IIT Delhi, he found things were different at the mess. Mess worker

Budhiya Ji was wearing a green T-shirt tucked instead of his blue uniform. The mess was painted, and the workers seemed trained. Budhiya Ji smiled but did not greet him with a pat on his back.

Tissues were placed near the plates. The number of glasses and spoons was more. Neil went inside the mess and asked the head cook about what happened.

"Neil Beta, where were you? Everything is changed. Now we are not your employees but of that giant caterer."

"Giant caterer? Mess is controlled by a caterer now?"

"Yes. We have been taught how to behave with you while serving the food. How to wear the cap while preparing the food. We have been instructed to close the mess sharp at 9:30 PM. You will not be able to barge in at 10 PM now and ask for food. Our supervisor tastes the food and asks to put less salt, less sugar. You tell me, how many years we have been serving you guys, *Beta*? You go. Your generation cannot be trusted."

It did not take much time for Neil to understand what happened during his absence.

*

One Sunday afternoon, Neil took Arjun to a street, three kilometres away from campus, towards the farms. He went straight to a small hut, outside of which some ladies were tying *jhaadu*, children were running here and there, and an old man was smoking a *beedi*, sitting on a coat. He saw Neil and threw his *beedi* away and came forward to greet him.

"How are you, Bhanu *Bhaisa*?"

"Your grace, Neil *Beta*. This time we are getting better prices with the help of your cooperative for our vegetables."

"That's great." Neil smiled.

"Meet my friend, Arjun." Neil pointed his right hand towards

Arjun and stared right into the eyes of the old man.

"Arjun, *Rakshas*?"

"No, no… He is not the rakshas."

Arjun had no clue what was going on.

"Bring that *Rakshas* here, and I will make sure he does not go back alive. He has no sense of humanity and fairness. Like a *Rakshas*, fully engrossed in his pride, he has stolen our means to earn bread and butter," the old man's eyes turned red.

*

"*Rakshas*?" Arjun looked towards Neil. "Neil, I get what he might be referring to, but how am I responsible for this? It is the vendor's choice to procure vegetables, where they get competitive prices." The old man's anger and his words, 'Arjun, *Rakshas*' were constantly buzzing in his mind.

They stopped at a tea shop.

"Arjun, local vendors have local contacts, and the relation-ship is just not professional. It is social and psychological, too, as they live here. With the caterer coming into the picture, local vendors are out of the equation. Previously, it was an ecosystem that developed near BITS. Now, it is pure business. Local vendors provided higher margins to local producers, which a caterer will not. The cost of food would become less, but students would be charged the same amount, and most of the margin would go into the caterer's pocket. The old man was pissed because, for the last 20 years, they have been relying on the students for the consumption of their product with good returns. Now it's like we have ditched them, and the culprit is you, because you are the face of the Student Union."

Arjun was looking down.

"But I did not intend this. My pride did not prompt me to opt for a better and hygienic system, Neil; it was required. It's my sensitivity. I am not a *Rakshas.*"

"Certainly, you are not, Arjun. A coin has two faces: one has value and the other has power and authority, but the whole coin is valuable." Neil smiled.

The remark by the strange old man could have been easily ignored, had it not been for Arjun. He thought over and over about it, the whole night. How many times might he have ignored the other side of the table and used his authority to derive biased decisions? But how could he do justice to both sides? But, as Neil mentioned, in the process of standardizing the mess, he completely ignored what value the ad hoc mess process was carrying. In the absence of a measuring metric, an unorganized process cannot be discarded. He visited ANC. The wall of the food counter had been raised up so that the preparation of food was not visible. *Does this mean proper hygiene? Previously, when the kitchen was visible, the cook had a fear of being noticed, and now they don't have that regular scrutiny.* What made him so sure about his decisions: his ego or his anger or something else he was not aware of himself? The thought almost made him shiver. He came back to his room, made some phone calls, and left the campus, leaving a note for Neil:

"Thanks, Neil, for being so kind to me, but I need to discover myself. Will call you once I find myself. Don't try to find me until then."

*

After three long yet seemingly short years, Arjun called Neil from China, and Neil reached there without any delay.

Neil smiled at his old buddy. Arjun smiled back. His eyes glinted, and he hugged Neil.

"Dude, I know there are questions to answer, but let me thank you first for making me realize what I am." Arjun sat beside

Neil on the bed in the house he had been living in under 'Karma Cult'.

"Is this you, Arjun, living with these bozos? You are certainly not a bozo." Neil laughed.

"I am not." Arjun laughed along.

"But these people are also not bozos, Neil. They are on a path of self-discovery here. Some of them are high office bearers in government as well as corporations. Some are athletes, some are knowledge seekers, and some are here out of curiosity, just like me when I joined," Arjun said.

"And what are they doing here?" asked Neil.

"Searching for peace. A lifestyle that would bring peace. I have been here for three years now. The old man who called me a *Rakshas*; his words worked as a torch, and it showed me my whole journey. You helped to bring out the bright side of me, but I still felt like something was missing. I also got to know about 'The Flipside Cult' project you have been working on through a mutual friend, and I really think what I found out here can help you, too, in your project. Consumerism cannot be the only external force making the world biased. Our existence cannot be just a reflection of the outer world. There has to be some other realm that we are missing in the engine, which helps resist these external forces and brings our own personality into the world. The world should be our reflection, Neil, us not of the world's. Neil, this is the only thing missing in your engine. Currently, the engine is focusing on the external forces, but it also needs to tell that change comes from within. You can show them how much some activity is productive or consumptive; this would help them discard the ones that are too consumptive. Stay here for some time and you will realize on your own, the power of performing productive activities and cutting down consumptive activities."

"Very well. I have six months. But then you are coming with me to work with me forever."

"Of course, I am."

*

In the next hearing, Arjun and Apanna did not come alone. There was a man with them. His face was covered with a white scarf and sunglasses. He was tall and broad. He sat near Apanna.

"Begin the proceeding," said Justice Singh, looking at the tall man, clearly an outlier there.

Arjun started the proceedings. "My Lord, this case is special. An internet-based search engine is accused of spreading anti-national sentiments about the government and the army. As explained earlier, the conclusions are based on historical events and the theory of ICT. On what basis the engine has come up with a conclusion, i.e., all historical events as well as the step-by-step fitting around the ICT algorithm, I have already provided the documentation to the court. Today, I brought a man with me who is a true testimony, relevant to this case."

"You can proceed with the case, Mr. Arjun."

Today, there were more people in the hearing. Arjun could hear more claps as he finished the last sentence.

"My Lord, our soldiers are our pride. Their blood flows in the veins of the country, and hence, the country is alive. But there is a difference between the army and the soldiers. I would like to invite Rtd. Colonel Rudra Pratap Singh to the witness box."

"Permission granted."

"Colonel RP Singh, give us a brief history of your work with the Indian Army."

"Respected Your Honor, I am Rtd Colonel Rudra Pratap Singh. I served as Colonel from 1989 to 2000, posted in Kashmir."

The man had grey eyes and a husky voice.

"This was the time when the neighboring country's interest in Kashmir was at its peak, and they supported terrorist activities with full intensity. Before 1987 and after 2004, the interest was not much because of different reasons. Your Honor, I am here not to speak in favor of or against the engine, but the truth has to be unveiled. This is an opportunity for me and all of us to contribute to a bigger revolution. I hope we all are able to see that. Let me explain what constitutes an army. The army is an institution headed by the President of India. Most of us perceive the army as an 'executing' unit, but practically it is a 'strategic' unit. The primary mission of the Indian Army is to ensure national security and national unity, defending the nation from external aggression and internal threats, and maintaining peace and security within its borders. The President is just a rubber stamp, and most of the strategic decisions for the army are taken by the ruling government. I repeat the ruling government, and the saddest part about our political system is—Democracy of India. My Lord, the government is elected every five years. India is not its government but its constitution. The government is faithful to its own rule, My Lord."

"Objection, My Lord. This is clearly his perception, and nothing concrete is being conveyed by the colonel." Adil Salem almost jumped off his chair.

"Objection overruled. Please continue, Colonel."

"Thank you, My Lord. The government is just faithful to its own rule. I always thought my soldiers sacrificed for India, but who is India, My Lord? Is it the government or the constitution? When I say I am an 'Indian', who do I pledge to? Very late in my life, My Lord, I realized that it's the people who make India. It's the people here, breathing within the Indian boundaries. After I myself killed hundreds of civilians in Kashmir, in Chhattisgarh, in Nagaland, my soul started questioning my patriotism, My Lord. I took early retirement, but still, my memories would not let me sleep with many questions unanswered. Ten years after I killed 20 men and 5 children in Kashmir, an audiotape leaked, and after listening to the audio, I realized that an army is a strategic unit not just to protect the integrity of India, but to help the ruling government win the confidence of voters. I clearly remember the conversation the two politicians had."

*

"The party is being condemned for the inefficient American weapons we purchased. The army has a huge emotional touch with the voters. If our image becomes anti-army, we might lose a potential share of votes."

"Then get the army on our side. This is not the first time, is it?"

"What about Pak terrorism? Kill some people on the border?"

"That's boring. Insurgency is the new trend. Get some people killed in the center of the state. This would attract media to a new issue, and voters would commend the government for its bold move."

"But what about the situation in the state? We might encounter real insurgency after the incident."

"How much voting proportion does the state contribute? And we would settle the insurgency after coming to power again."

"As you command, PM."

*

"My Lord, I started researching all insurgency cases and selectively focused on the ones that happened near election time. Most of them were in Kashmir, and others included Naxalites and BODO in Nagaland. Not all insurgency cases were fake; many of them were genuine, but I cannot stand the idea of the army being used for political advantage. The army is very powerful. Just look at the neighboring country. How powerful is the army there, and what consequences it may face if misguided? That's all I have, My Lord. Thank you."

"Mr. Adil, do you have any questions for the colonel?"

"I sure do, Your Honor."

"Colonel RP Singh, do you feel you have ever done anything that was not described as your duty as per the constitution?"

"No."

"Do you have some psychological disorder?"

"No."

"No, Colonel, you do have a mental disorder. It's called 'Delusion'." Adil Salem abruptly turned to Justice Singh. "My Lord, Inquiries were set up, and everybody came out clean in all the cases he has mentioned. Whatever he has said is just his perception, and there are no facts to it. I ask the court to disqualify such witnesses in the future, and let the engine be banned forever. That's all, My Lord."

The court went silent. The judge was writing something in her journal.

"Mr. Arjun, can you please help us understand how the particular story told by Colonel approves of ICT, on which your engine is based?" asked Justice Singh.

The question was the least expected. Even Arjun and Apanna were taken aback, but it shocked Adil the most. He was convinced that the engine was going to lose the case in the absence of firm evidence, and the colonel's story was subdued by his argument. He adjusted his coat.

"Your Honor, consumerism, when defined individually, is a desire for more and more. In the engine, identities are not just personal but political, social, and economic. For political identity, consumerism is about seeking more and more power by a particular entity. For social identity, consumerism is seeking more and more recognition, and for economic identities, it is seeking more and more wealth. Here, in this case, ideally, the government should not have used the army for its own interest. The ruling government wanted more power. It's sheer consumerism, My Lord."

Justice Singh took half an hour before she stopped writing and looked at the curious audience.

"This case is for sure special and will be treated specially. Generally, when there are multiple cases against someone, the verdict for each case is given separately by the court. For the cases against The Flipside Cult, this is how it will be dealt with. The first case does not close today, though there will not be any hearing hereafter on this case. After hearing for all the cases have been finished, the final verdict will be given in the end. All who filed the cases, either they all lose or they all win. There won't be a case-by-case verdict. The potential the engine carries to make an impression on the masses is very powerful, and we have all seen that already. The court removes the ban today on the engine and directs the engine not to suggest any relationship between established powerful entities, which have a nationwide public appearance, until the final verdict is provided. The list of those entities would be provided later by the court. Hearings for the engine will be prioritized above all hearings pending in this court, as this is a matter of national integrity. The court is adjourned for today."

Adil Salem was not happy, but Apanna and Arjun were. The army man looked concerned.

*

"I am happy the way Justice Singh made the decision." Apanna relaxed her legs on the couch in her apartment in Delhi.

"Me too. Though we are supposed to fight until the last case, and then only the verdict on the ban will be given. But yeah, declaring a win or a loss in cases sequentially would have impacted the faith of people in the engine and may have dampened the increasing craze about the engine," Arjun said, stretching his hands on the recliner.

"True. By the way, what do you think Justice Singh is up to? Does she believe in us? Why would she go unconventionally for us?" Apanna again lay on the sofa, talking to the roof.

"I think she wants to help us, within the system. I believe she agrees with ICT theory; she just wants to see, whether the engine goes along with the theory, and for that, she will be hearing the cases one by one, and by the end, if she is convinced, she might give a verdict which would create history." Arjun smiled.

"I guess we are underestimating Justice Singh's intellect and oversimplifying her intention. She is not writing case files, Apanna. She is writing a testimony for the cult. Let's try to explain to the court as much as possible." Arjun shouted like he had just discovered something very exclusive about Justice Singh.

*

There were almost 50 people in the court attending the trial for the second case. Justice Singh's last hearing was covered in the media, and it became a viral topic on social media.

Adil Salem was sitting with the NHCI representative. Arjun and Apanna took the same place they had in the last hearing.

"Start the proceeding, Prosecutor," said Justice Singh as she entered the court.

"Your Honor, how did you come to the court today?" asked Adil Salem.

"In my car, of course."

"What if your car gets punctured in the middle of the road, or there is a traffic jam, or your car's tire is stuck in a pothole?"

"Then you would have less time today for your case," Justice Singh said with a straight face. Laughter spread across the hall.

"Right, My Lord. It is very important to maintain the road infrastructure in a highly loaded environment. For that, the NHCI gives the contract to highly competitive firms that make sure that the highways are well-engineered and finished on time, as they are the veins of the nation, and the flow should be uninterrupted. There are very few firms, My Lord, which can accomplish this complex engineering project, and often the contract for big projects is given to selected entities. To-day's case is about the engine's flipside relationship of GCK Corporation with NHCI, claiming that GCK is earning a very uncompetitive ROI on its highway investments, and NHCI is partial and biased in its highway project allocation process and has not followed the right measures for revenue collection.

The current model is like this: Some amount is given by the government as an advance to the firm, and the remaining amount is recovered by the firm from the public via toll tax. Over a prescribed period, the firm charges toll tax, and the firm is responsible for the maintenance of the highway for that period. The total cost incurred by the company is not just the fixed contract amount, but the variable amount incurred in repairs over a period of time. This total fixed and variable cost is then recovered via toll tax. These kids are applying class five Mathematics here and accusing the NHCI of selectively giving the contracts to their favorites with very unreasonable

ROI. They are not considering the cost they incur over a period of time." Adil Salem finished his argument in one go.

"Mr. Arjun, you have something in defense?"

"Thank you, My Lord. Certainly not every firm that applies for big highway projects should be considered competent and allocated the projects. I also agree that when we calculate the ROI, variable costs should be included with the fixed one, and I am sure the engine did not include the repair cost in lieu of the unavailability of data. But, My Lord, let's not just assume something and come to a conclusion, unlike my friend Adil Salem. The power of assumption is that they are common between you, me, and everyone. They are the easiest tool to win confidence and fool people."

Arjun was louder today than he was in the previous hearings. Some audiences clapped when he paused, and some waited for more drama to unfold.

"Senior Prosecutor, let me show you how class five Mathematics can challenge your assumptions. My Lord, let me first explain how the engine came up with the conclusion."

The audience was absolutely hooked. Adil Salem and the judge, too, seemed curious to know what he was about to show.

"The firm GCK has built five highways in India, My Lord. Since both GCK and NHCI are specific firms, there is nothing much to explain about how the engine first positioned them. In the data collection part, the engine gathers all past data regarding GCK and NHCI. The first highway that GCK built was 30 years ago in northeast India—a 700 km long highway. This was not based on the current revenue model. At that time, a contract amount was signed and no long-term maintenance or toll collection was in the contract. They took almost three years to finish the project. This is the worst project by the firm, with highway conditions more pathetic than the state highways in the region. The highway was criticized across the northeast media, but somehow it did not catch the heat in the national media. The next two projects to build 1,000 km long highways in central India were given while the firm was building its first highway. The firm had been involved in the construction of many other public projects. But the scale of highway projects was much bigger than any other project the firm ever took up. When the first highway did not turn out to be successful, the media started condemning the firm while they were constructing the second and the third highways. These highways were also on the same revenue model. At that time, another firm, Gati, which constructed very robust highways, pitched to take up others, but its application was discarded. Rather, a contract for repair was also given to GCK later. They constructed bad quality highways and then repaired and charged the government for their uncompetitive work..." Arjun suddenly stopped upon listening to Adil Salem's objection.

"Objection, My Lord. The construction technology was not as competitive at that time. But now you see the latest two projects by GCK are exceptional. The quality is good, and moreover, the NHCI made the current revenue model, which includes the contract of repairing the highways along with the construction itself. Everyone learned to make a sustainable environment."

"Objection overruled."

"Thank you, My Lord. Point to be noted: when they were not responsible for the repairs, the construction was of very bad quality, which needed more repair in the following course of time. On the contrary, when they are made responsible for the repair, the quality is so good that hardly any repair work is required. On top of it, they collect toll tax over a prolonged period of time in the new model. This is pure corruption, My Lord. So entities like competitors, highways, construction material, etc., are part of the ICT model, which then predicts the relationship. And in this case, clearly, GCK is a consumer to whom NHCI is a provider. NHCI is a public entity, and being biased towards a private firm for the projects makes this entire entity questionable."

Hall echoed with people's murmurs.

"As the senior prosecutor himself said that highly sensitive projects cannot be offered to just anyone. When 30 years ago the GCK firm pitched for its first highway project, what was the basis? Another firm that was involved in highway building and had accomplished many other successful projects, not just in India, but abroad too, was rejected based on its slightly higher quote. Furthermore, why does NHCI continue to allocate the projects to GCK, in spite of the sub-standard quality of work?

For the last two projects, some foreign firms also bid, with quotes less than the firm's. Still, GCK was allocated the high-cost projects on the basis of its rapport with NHCI. My Lord, in the second model, where the firm is supposed to collect toll and repair the damages, the revenue to the firm, to date, is 20 times more than it used to be in the previous model, and the repair work is minimal. NHCI may have selected the model to make the construction firms practically answerable for the damages and take corrective action, but this model is making millions for the firm, and the revenue is being generated at toll booths, with public money. Ideally, toll collection should not have been extended beyond the 10-year period, but it has been 15 years, and the firm is still filling its pocket with public money. Here is the 'Class Five' calculation to support the facts I mentioned."

Arjun handed over a file to the judge and sipped some water.

"The language is mine, but facts are the engine's, My Lord. Some facts I got from the RTI, which support the engine's claim." Arjun made his closing statement and sat along with Apanna peacefully.

"As you know, there is no verdict in this special case, but I close it today. No further hearings will be made on this particular case." Justice Singh addressed the audience.

*

The way things were moving for The Flipside Cult, for Apanna, it was miraculous. She had been in court case hearings before, and she knew how things moved practically. It was like even the universe was trying to support The Flipside Cult. Or it was Neil, united into the infinity, doing all this! Right from the Congo trip till very recently, both Neil and Apanna communicated through emails, very often. The mails that she could access whenever she wanted, and read Neil himself or herself sharing about their bond, about the cult, about Arjun and Veera, or just about themselves.

Dear Neil,

I hope you have left Congo and reached the US safely. Why don't you visit India sometime? We will spend some quality time together. Walk along Marine Drive, eat rolls in Khan Market, trek in Sikkim. See, I have so many plans for us! But as I know, you must be busy developing and making the engine robust. Forget the last-to-last sentence, I tend to throw some tantrums at times, never mind. I truly respect what you are doing, the bigger picture that you have in your mind.

You asked me whether I wanted to join the team to help the engine get publicized. Yes, I want to be on the team. Neil, I feel the engine is mature enough. It's the wisest man with no eyes. It has got its unique philosophy, brilliant computing power on data, competent logic, and also a team. I have published an article for the same.

Though I understand how things work for the engine, I will be needing your input on technicalities for my next article.

PS: Do let me know the story behind the name 'The Flipside Cult'.

Until next time.

Yours only,

Apanna

6

The Leaf in the Machine

Veera did not have a smooth stay in Congo. Though she always wanted to work on the African land as an activist, Congo offered an altogether different set of challenges to her. There was mafia, and she had to keep a low profile there.

Congolese were not anymore the sons of the first men. It was a developing country. She landed at the airport at Makabana, a southern town lying at the edge of the Kouilou-Niari River.

She made a few friends who were university students there, through Facebook and introduced herself as an MIT graduate turned travel blogger, and her purpose there was to meet African students and learn about modern Africa. Students there could speak English, and some of them had been to India as exchange students, and Veera sometimes played badminton with them.

A few kilometers from the main township, towards the river, she captured the beauty of the African continent on her camera. It was a paradise to her. The landscapes you would not find anywhere else but in Africa. The net of rivers spreading across the continent, making the veins, which nurtured the green land

and different colors on the continent.

She spent a month wandering around the Republic of Congo. She could almost sketch a map of Congo, both geographical and political. To the civilians, she was just another travel blogger, but to herself, she was a bomb of justice to be exploded soon in the land of injustice.

While traveling, she made sure to eat dinner with a journalist, to share a hotel with an activist, and trek with student groups. She was good at managing different networks of people.

Somehow, the university students at a local university arranged a keynote speech from her at their convocation ceremony at the university as she belonged to prestigious MIT and was a published travel blogger and an environmentalist with almost a million visitors to her YouTube channel. She was invited to deliver a speech on the evolving Africa and students' role in it.

Hmm, a place where dignitaries would be present, and I will be on stage; good time to execute, thought Veera and accepted the invitation.

On the day of convocation, Veera, wearing a pair of blue jeans and a black top with her hair tucked into a bun behind, came to the stage and took the mic in hand.

"I know no student would want to come and study here at this university." The way Veera looked at the audience, most of them could not believe the audacious statement she began with. "I mean, look around you. What you have got! It's nature's paradise around, and who would want to barter a deep sleep under a big tree with a class on the university campus, ha?" The hall roared with laughter.

"Africa! It has no alternative in the whole world. It is nature's heaven. But you know what! I feel that hard work in this university is more important for Congolese than leisure in the continent. You must learn to preserve what God has gifted you, and that can only be achieved with the right education. Let me ask you a question: What makes our food tasty? Its ingredients, right! What makes Africa look beautiful? Its resources under the land. If you don't have good spices and ingredients, the food won't taste good. Similarly, if the resources are stolen, the land won't look beautiful anymore. It would be barren land with all its essence stolen by someone else. This is where the role of education comes, my friends. This is no longer the first men's era. There are political boundaries, and people have to protect the sovereignty of their country from outsiders. Education helps disintegrate and analyze the situation to its root causes. It makes you see the practical boundaries that we humans have created. It is to train your brain for the practical world because there is no other choice. My friend is here from the local NGO group "Save Africa", who will show you a documentary on how the outsiders are spoiling African beauty, stealing its resources. Thank you." Veera came down from the podium, leaving the audience awestruck and the university dean and the local mining firm's MD, who came as chief guests, dumbstruck.

The university dean looked surprisingly at the student and faculty organizer for what had just happened, as he did not expect something good to come out of the documentary. The front row in the auditorium was occupied by the dean, HRD minister of the Republic of Congo as the Chief Guest, accompanied by Paul Lee, Continent Head of 'Zhou Minerals', which had the greatest number of mines in Congo. The consequences of anything going wrong would be very bad, he thought. The dean signaled the organizer to proceed to the next speaker, but it was late, and the documentary had already started introducing

Zhou Minerals and its widespread network of mines in Congo. Involved in a variety of mineral mining, Zhou Minerals has generated employment for thousands of Congolese.

After 30 seconds, the documentary started focusing on the local people working for Zhou Minerals, and Veera's voice started leading the documentary.

"Let's ask these people only what change was promised and what it brought."

An old man is seen on the screen.

"For how long have you been working here?"

"It's been almost five years."

"Do you get paid? Do you have a home to live in?"

"Yes, everything is taken care of by the company. The company is good."

"Was there no company here five years ago? What were you doing then to earn money?"

"We did not allow any company. We grew bananas and sold them in Makabana. This company has been with us for five years, and we trust the company."

Focus from the old man then shifted to a child.

"What do you do here?" asked the leading voice to the child.

"My mom works, and there is no one at home to take care of me, so I come along with her."

"Ok, but what do you do here all day?"

"I sit on the mountain there and see the land, and try to hit the first tree with my slingshot."

"Are you able to hit the trees?"

"There is no tree in my slingshot's range. Earlier, I used to easily find a tree nearby and be able to hit it, but now they are too far. Just near the river. My mom says the mountain is shifting."

The focus is shifted from the child to the mountains nearby, and the leading voice said, "And the mountains have started to drift now. Ridiculous, isn't it? There is no education system here maintained for the children to let them know that mountains don't shift, but trees may dry and land may become barren. The company's pact was to use only the barren land, and the company has stuck to its vows. Then why is the barren land area increasing every year, and the jungle is getting out of range of a little child's slingshot? Clearly, there is no education for children, and the company looks at them as future potential workers. 'Miner's Village' was known as 'The Banana Village' before the company started working here," the leading voice says, showing an older clip when banana production was the main occupation. "With a population of around 5,000, the village is now solely dependent on the mining company, not just in terms of earning, but food supply, water, and sanitation. Everything is good about the company except, there is nothing good about it. Shrill music starts playing in the background.

The land is systematically being made barren to establish more mining facilities. Until a year back, the company used to supply water cans with a red label, which has changed to blue now. The red labeled water had a chemical Phyloxin-BX , which, via human waste, went to rivers, was soluble in groundwater, absorbed via plant roots, mimicked plant hormones, slowly disrupted the vascular system, and ultimately wiped-off the jungle. The process was gradual. The chemical was routed to trees for three to four years, and now, when the company has got enough barren land, they have stopped serving 'red labeled' water cans."

The leading voice stopped, and a black screen appeared. "I am Veera Ganesan, and I have been in Africa for a couple of weeks to find out about the inhumane activities in the Congo Republic. The reports of ground soil have been sent to the UN along with samples of water, which were used to be served a year ago. Thanks to the

African culture of storing water, we were lucky to find one can in the basement of one of the families in 'Village of Bananas'. Let's save all other 'Village of Bananas' from becoming the 'Village of Miners'."

The documentary ended with everyone awestruck. Veera had already left the ceremony while the documentary was playing. Everybody was kind of scared about the consequences except for one person, a local reporter Laco, a part-time BBC reporter.

Just ten seconds before Veera announced that she was going to show a documentary there, electricity ran through his body. He thought a lot in just 10 seconds. *What does she have to show here? A video, some photographs? How did she manage to get it? I have been trying for years, but never succeeded. But, on top of all, with the company head and government ministers here, will she be able to escape the continent after this?* After the documentary ended, he went to his lodge and knocked on a door, which surely was not the entrance to his room.

"Ms. Veera, please open the gate." He knocked on the door twice.

"Ms. Veera, I am not a cop, believe me, let me in," said Laco, breathing fast.

Veera looked through the peephole and opened the gate.

"Please, Mr. Laco, come in." Veera smiled.

"I saw you yesterday in this lodge, Ms. Veera, but how the hell do you know me?" asked Laco, entering the room.

"You are a famous BBC reporter, aren't you?" Veera laughed.

Laco was looking at Veera with wide eyes and a grin.

"Ok, sorry, let me come to the point. Why do you think, Mr. Laco, you were invited to the convocation 100 miles away?"

"Did you ask Kimo to invite me?"

Veera nodded her head, smiling. Kimo was the Student Union

president and a new friend and supporter of Veera.

"You like to cover international issues, right, Mr. Laco? I am sure you found a very good material here."

"How? By sending your documentary to the BBC? Well, I have covered the whole event there. I can do that."

"What do you think, Mr. Laco? BBC does not have this data? It's a conspiracy. They won't publish it. Do you know why I was not put down there? First, the company wants to keep its clean image, and second, the company knows that people like me come and go, and the business continues. But I am not just anyone. You are not sending the documentary to the BBC."

"Why did you show it then? If it does not come out, what is the purpose?"

"Why do you think I did not post this on some viral YouTube channel?"

"Maybe you don't have a viral YouTube channel."

"Well, I can pay, and any viral channel would post anything I want. The reason is that Africa is not the same anymore. The revolution has to come from inside. Outsiders can show sympathy, but the locals only will know the pain. This time, the revolt should come from the inside. I showed it to the students of Africa. Young blood is more powerful. I have a strategy in place, and I need your help. I leave this continent today, and you are going to help the engine develop here."

"Wait, wait, first thing, you are leaving?"

"The only way to do groundwork against the government or a big corporate here is by keeping a low profile. I am exposed. But not you or 'The Flipside Cult'. You don't write an article to BBC now. We will be in touch. Just keep your profile low and help to build the cult."

"The Flipside Cult?"

"Yes, 'The Flipside Cult'. Sit here. Will explain to you everything."

*

Dearest Apanna,

Welcome to the Cult! We all are happy that the Cult has traveled offshore, and Arjun and Veera can't wait to meet you. Veera will be visiting her hometown next month. I hope you guys catch up sometime. For your next article, I have prepared a story, which you might find a little philosophical, but trust me, the ICT (Integrated Consumerism Theory) is much easier to understand after reading this, and here it goes:

Initially, Earth was not overly populated with humans, and it was balanced with a number of species across the food chain. The original source of energy is the Sun, and it was mostly populated by the plants at the bottom of the food pyramid. The population of species went down as we moved upstream in the food chain. Air, water, land—everything was distributed in a balance, and the ecosystem worked at its best in a harmonious style.

Now, from there to present, the way the food chains evolved, everybody thinks human intellect is the reason behind, but actually, it was something else. It was his fear of pain and also his high empathy for similar humans, which multiplied the fear of pain. Humans could feel pain in other humans' suffering, while this empathy factor was not as high in other animals. These two factors led humans to live in groups, and humans evolved as social animals. There were other animals too, which evolved as social animals, but what made humans different from the other animals was the ability of humans to compromise. Compromise on freedom. You could see a lone wolf wandering in its ego, but lone humans were rare to trace. This indeed helped humans to save their lives, and the human population started growing. With an increased population, the food chain got skewed. They needed more food and more shelter. They started positioning themselves at each level of the food chain. They started consuming almost every living being in the food chain. Agriculture developed, fire was invented, and a culture started forming around the very basic idea—living in a group. And groups gave everything to humans but complete emotional freedom. Compromise is the death of freedom.

As a social animal with a large population, humans were able to deal with external threats, but internal stability became the most challenging task for them and fundamental problem was the same— compromising with individual freedom. As society they developed, but as an individual, they failed big time.

But not everybody compromised to the same degree. Fearlessness was a determining factor in deciding who would hold the command in the group. The most capable person would make the laws, and the remaining would abide by the laws. This brought into life the class system in human societies. The ones making the laws, enjoying freedom the most, kept hold of the resources, in short, holding the power became the 'owner' class, and those who compromised the most became the 'slavery' class, or today what we call them as 'powerful people' and 'public', respectively. The irony here is that out of the total human population, the upper classes or the powerful people, make up just 10 percent. The remaining 90 percent is the class that does not know what its identity is. We may call it the middle class and the poor class. It's not about heredity, but about acceptance: where do you want to settle? Humans accept unconditionally that the classes exist. Yesterday's richest may not be today's wealthiest man, but we accept the idea of wealth disparity. Since powerful people with more wealth are perceived to exercise more freedom, we learned to create, keep, and grow wealth, as today's idea of exercising freedom is more and more wealth leading to more and more consumption. Now, we don't aspire for the freedom that nature held for us millions of years ago, but for the freedom to consume more. The more resources we have to consume, the freer we feel, as it makes us feel that we hold control over resources. This idea of more and more consumption to feel free is very powerful and widespread.

The engine's central idea is—try to fit the relationships and activities around the idea of consumerism, as it is the present time's spouse of freedom, which is the most desired emotion/feeling of any living being. Deep down, all forces work in one direction—attaining freedom, for now and for the future. There are algorithms involved, details of which are there on the engine. Engine's idea is centralized around consumerism, but the goal is the flip side of consumerism. What if we did not choose to compromise our individual freedom and accepted pain? The answer to be revealed in the following years.'

I hope the above story is eligible to be in your column. Regarding the name 'The Flipside Cult', sync up with Veera, as she was the one to suggest it. Very interesting.

Take care and love me.

Your love,

Neil

*

In India, the engine was becoming famous across the country. Since the engine was not allowed to suggest a relationship between the entities mentioned in the court's list, people started introspecting their choice of activities in their daily routine. An article about this went viral on Facebook.

"I am an engineer by profession in Bengaluru. I have seen people in my family earning 20,000–30,000 a month. Even my

Hindi teacher, who spotted the talent in me and helped me make a show out of it, also worked for a 40,000 monthly pay cheque. Earning 3–4 times that amount a month is for sure a feeling of achievement for me, and trust me, this is good enough to live a metro lifestyle. I was happily living my life until what The Flipside Cult showed me. Two weeks ago, I got to know about the controversial platform 'The Flipside Cult', which shows how much any activity is productive or consumptive. Firstly, I put my basic information in the engine, and as stated in the document on its homepage, the engine positioned me in its multidimensional identity space. It showed me statistically where I stand politically, economically, and socially across all users using The Flipside Cult. I was positioned slightly beyond the median position, a happy moment for a man who belonged to a middle-class family. It then asked me my regular activities, i.e., social, economic, and political transactions I did on average. Where did I spend my money, what shows I watched, what has been my savings, what properties I owned, how frequently I visited my hometown, how much time I spent with my own family, choice of entertainment, etc., and many other questions. In the end, the engine showed how many of my activities are consumptive or motivated by consumerist forces. I was shocked by the results. Not because it showed that 80 percent of my time and 60 percent of my money went into consumptive activities, but the fact that my choices were common to most of the people, positioned near me. Have we become so predictable and lost our uniqueness in the darkness of consumerism that the choices we make are not unique but common? Is someone else controlling our choices? My Hindi teacher always believed that I was unique, but the engine tells me the flipside story—uniqueness is an illusion in the world we are living in now; we have just one identity—'Consumers', positioned at different levels of economic scale. With everyone spending a lot of time browsing social media, which is driven by an advertising motive, thought processes and ideas would originate in an almost similar context, in line with what has been promoted. With everyone running after brands, there is no uniqueness in the desire for some special fabric or leather or ingredients. It's all about mass following. We do what people do or what 'consumers' do. One fool, making a chain with another fool, and the whole world becomes a fool. I get the whole philosophy behind this consumerism. It starts with a desire for more money. I never felt that 40,000 a month was insufficient for my Hindi teacher in my town to run her household. But more money meant success. The more you earn, the more successful you are considered. Money undoubtedly brings more purchasing power, leisure, respect, etc., but there is no end to this race. We, humans, show off our success like trophies. There is a catch. You earn more only to become a consumer ultimately, and once your activities are mostly consumptive, your earnings stabilize. This is the point where you want to earn even more, but you won't be able to, because you are close to being a perfect 'consumer,' and consumers pay, they don't earn.

I am here to support this beautiful work by Neil Sengupta and his team. Please share how much the percentage is for you through the link below. This is for a good purpose; let's not fill in random numbers. Currently, the engine is going through a very tough time, and our support can help it a lot in its validation and approval. Let's be part of the change.

https://goo.gl/12dfl4

• Avnit Basu"

"The article went viral, Arjun. I don't even know this guy, and why the hell these corporations are silent with no attempt to discourage what is going on," said Apanna while selecting which song to play in the car Arjun drove, taking them both for a long ride.

"Haha, make it a habit, Apanna, the Cult will be going farther, but yeah, not farther from where Neil envisioned it. I guess Justice Singh played it right. Big corporations don't care. They are born out of selfish ideology to make the most of resources to add to their profit."

"Do you know how many responses this guy has had until now? Any guesses?"

"Maybe one million."

"Ten million, man! Ten million! And all of them reported 80 percent consumptive activities. I wish we could present it to Justice Singh."

"Don't you think she already knows it?" Arjun smiled and raised the volume of the song.

*

Dear love,

Do you miss me often these days, as lately, I have been missing you badly? When two hearts can stay connected across seas, why not their feelings? I am not going to ask you how you are, as I will be there in the US next week and will see for myself.

By the way, I did not know you were such a fantastic storyteller. The last article about the philosophy behind the engine was taken with a huge interest among the public. I am happy that the number of Indian users has increased after that. I get compliments for that article in mail and in person, not just from our age, but from the elderly, too. It's a very well-received article in India, as far as my understanding goes about the Indian mindset. People also complimented me on the story behind the name 'The Flipside Cult', which I got to know from Veera. Now, when I think what it could have been if not The Flipside Cult, the answer always is 'nothing but The Flipside Cult'. It must have changed the NGO volunteers' lifestyle, who worked for the engine at MIT, so much that the engine became the new religion for them. But how could a by-product of science be a religion? Hence, it was named a cult, and since it showed the other side of the coin, it became 'The Flipside Cult', what a name!

I must say Veera is a badass girl, man! She is very good at networking and very determined for her purpose. Let me tell you what happened! We met at a roadside café outside DU, and there, she happened to notice a student street drama with hundreds of people as the audience. In no time, she went and talked to the organizers and got herself a chance to demonstrate a biodegradable tissue paper made out of a fabric that dries in a few minutes. She gave everyone an online link to buy it. This tissue paper would save money, trees, and serve the purpose. She gave me one, too. She happened to meet a junior from her college, who was working with the company that made this tissue, just an hour before we met, how cool is that!

I am happy to be part of the awesome team, Neil. Thanks for being in my life. Will see you next week there.

Yours only,

Apanna

*

Most of the crowd at the court this time belonged to the millennial generation.

Justice Singh entered.

"Please start the proceeding, Prosecutor."

Salem stood up and stepped forward to begin.

"The engine has been accused of spreading anti-national sentiments across the public by showing the relationship between the public and the USBI bank as 'Public being looted by USBI Bank, ultimately serving big tycoons with loan defaulting.' My Lord, USBI is a public bank. Crores of people in this country, including the rich and the poor, have their savings accounts in the bank, and daily transaction is about 1,000 crore rupees through retail banking. The bank has its branches all over India as well as in countries like South Africa, Dubai, Bangladesh, Nepal, Bali, etc. In brief, USBI plays a very crucial role in running the country's economy and commerce. Any rumors about corrupt management or inefficient handling of public money would shatter the economy. The stock price of the bank has halved since the engine's flipside relationship got viral. A lot of damage has already been done. Please, let's not let this destructive tool continue functioning out there in public anymore. Thank you, Your Honor."

"Mr. Arjun Shastri. Do you have anything to defend?"

"Oh yes, My Lord, otherwise what purpose would I serve to the court." Arjun stood up, laughing.

"Your Honor, when I was hearing Advocate Salem, I remembered an incident that happened in my maternal village when I was 10. There was a public water storage tank built in the farm fields of the village's wealthiest man, whom we called 'Banna Ji'. He provided the land for the public tank. There was a public water tap from which villagers would take and store the water for various uses. Supply was once in four days for five hours, and the entire village stored water in their houses for drinking, cooking, and sanitary uses. It was also used to fill the tank, which served as a storage facility to provide drinking water to village animals, emergency uses, and for all needs in public places like temples. Since the tank was important, the agreement was that the tank should be at least half-filled on the day when the supply runs. So when water flowed in pipes, first it would go to the tank, and then villagers would store water for personal uses. There was harmony in the process until a drought hit the state. The water supply was cut down to once a week. Wells started drying. The village's crop did not do well except for Banna Ji's. Your Honor, here is the analogy—The water supply is the public money, which is being stored in a tank, which is the bank. Since banks earn through interest on loans, the big loan awardees become the Banna Ji, the base of banks. If, in some circumstances, Banna Ji, the big firms, turn into defaulter and are not able to return the money, the bank would be in a major deficit of cash, just like Banna Ji used the tank water for his fields, and emptied the tank. But it cannot become empty, as it has to feed others too, the economy has to run, so more public money would be injected to keep the tanks half-filled, or in other words, the banks full."

"Objection, My Lord. We need facts. We get the stories. We love stories. But, here we need facts."

"Objection overruled. Mr. Arjun, please continue!"

"Thanks, Your Honor. Valya's default was 9,000 crores for USBI. Just after the immediate quarterly result, they started charging one rupee as the ATM transaction fee. As Advocate Salem pointed out, there are crores of accounts in SBI, there are lakhs of transactions each day, My Lord. This is how the bank recovered its money. This is the whole game behind scaling. Technically, the bank did not lose the money, but it was a one-rupee donation to Valya every citizen paid, and who is the collector here? Our beloved USBI. This is not the only case, My Lord. This was big and came to the limelight, but there are thousands of default cases, the list of which is in this file. It is not like private banks don't have default cases. But they have a whistleblower on top. They have to answer to the shareholders. They care about their image, but they, too, are not averse to default. USBI is a channel of scaling. One rupee is not much for someone, but when aggregated over crores of people, it is a big amount. The proof for the facts is in the file, My Lord, kept on your desk. The Flipside Cult did not target USBI specifically. If searched, almost all the banks are infected with such malignancy."

"Mr Arjun, can you please suggest how the engine came up with the data and the conclusion?" asked Justice Singh.

"Sure, My Lord. USBI is a known entity, and the public represents a volume of average Indian citizens. This is how the engine has positioned them. In the data collection part, USBI has multiple partners, customers, and history. Government, big firms, public, loan rates, housing loans, saving accounts, etc., are some entities that are common with the public, and the engine puts all this in ICT modelling.

Let's take some examples in ICT modelling. Let's say in the first case, when it makes the Public as the provider and USBI as the consumer. Let's consider the big firms as an entity, being a consumer, USBI would like to gain as much from the entities, and this can be done by providing them more and more loans to gain interest. Now, big firms, with more loans, would charge more to the public. Public being a provider is paying for the interests, big firms are paying to banks. Let's consider another entity—savings accounts. Banks, being the consumers, would try to gain as much money as they can from the public and invest it to gain returns. The public, being the provider, would keep money in the savings accounts for as long as possible. Now let's merge these two. Banks are getting more and more money from the public to grant loans to big firms to earn interest. There are other entities, too, like loan rate, housing loans, government, etc., for which this simulation is done. Vice versa, the engine does simulation with USBI as the provider and the public as a consumer. Let's take housing loan as a simulation entity. Public, being a consumer, would take as much housing loan as they can and would default with ease. Similarly, savings rates would surpass the loan rates USBI has been charging. In the next step, the engine would test the above hypothesis with the historical data and would test which simulation has predicted more accurate results.

USBI, being the consumer, would show a positive correlation with the test data, as seen historically, banks have been providing more and more loans to businesses, and inflation is increasing. Now, when it's clear who is the consumer and who is the provider, with more historical data, it would come to a conclusion, and in this case, it suggests that banks are agents of big firms to loot public money and ultimately distribute it to those firms in a very legal and systematic manner. That's all, Your Honor."

"Interesting, do you have any questions, Advocate Salem?"

"Yes, My Lord. May I?"

"Sure."

"I want to invite Ms. Apanna to the witness box."

Apanna came to the witness box.

"Ms. Apanna, there are some facts presented in the document passed to the court regarding USBI bank, and you mentioned that you used RTI to get that information available here, right?"

"Objection, My Lord, this is not specific to this case. We have the right facts, and the court can verify. It does not matter how we got them." Arjun almost shouted.

"Objection overruled." Justice Singh fixed her specs.

"Thank you, Your Honour. Did you, Ms. Apanna?"

"Yes."

"When, may I ask?"

"I used to work in the Hind News, and I had a copy of those facts, which we retrieved from RTI."

"Or you stole the information, Ms. Apanna? My Lord, two days ago, Ms. Apanna went to her office and told the receptionist that she was there to collect her belongings. But she took a copy of the case she was investigating before without authorized permission. The in-charge is here for the testimony, and CCTV cameras tell the remaining story. She stole the information, My Lord, and Hind News has filed a case against her. Since this is also related to his case, I request the court to take it as criminal activity and take Ms Apanna's act as a serious crime, as it is impacting this case."

Arjun was sitting with his shoulders down and hands on his cheeks.

"Take Ms. Apanna Popat into custody until further notified by the court. We will take up the next case at the next hearing. The court is adjourned."

*

"Hi Apanna," Veera greeted Apanna, sitting behind the bars. Arjun just waved his hand with a grin.

"So, how is the dream place, Apanna?" Arjun tried to ease the moment.

"Well, more realistic than my first time," Apanna replied with a faint smile.

"How are things there, Veera? You were not reachable on your local number." Apanna came closer to the bars.

"Things are awesome, Apanna. Soon, we will hear back from Congo." Veera looked right into Apanna's eyes. They were red and proved that her smile was artificial.

The trio held each other's hands, and Arjun could spot tears in Apanna's eyes. Before the tears rolled down her cheeks, Arjun wiped them off with his palm.

"Apanna, as far as I know you, these are not for the bars standing between us. What is it making you so vulnerable here? I am getting anxious." Arjun crossed his fingers with Apanna's.

"No, it's just something on my mind." Apanna looked away. "I am behind bars, and I am not able to do anything from here. I want Neil's dream to come true, a utopian world, but I am not able to. I know you guys are out there, but it is just that I am overthinking about Neil here."

"He lives in us, Apanna. He lives in the engine and its power. There have been men of action before, but this man was a man of destiny. He pictured all this, how it's all going to happen. The engine is going to change the future, just a matter of time," Veera said in a determined voice.

"Oh, girl, what Africa has done to you, I am refueled!" Arjun tried to reset the sentiment of the moment, assisting Veera.

"Boy, you got it right, this is about what I have done to Africa," said Veera with a loud voice and intense stare.

Apanna's eyes were not faking smiles anymore. It was a smile in the hope of more true smiles.

*

"Sir, this is the last tape I copied that day, and here it is." Laco threw the tape into the dustbin.

"How do I know you don't have any other?" asked the university dean.

Laco made a face, suggesting the absurdity of such a question by the dean.

"I am a reporter with BBC. Don't you think I would have already sent the tape to BBC by now if I wanted to? I am a patriotic citizen of the Congo Republic. This is the last evidence of the documentary that the Indian girl made, and now it's in the dustbin. You have got bigger problems," Laco spoke, showing concern.

"Come close."

The dean moved forward.

"The girl is not the only problem. The bigger problem is 'The Flipside Cult'."

"The what?"

"The girl works for a product called 'The Flipside Cult'. Whatever she found out here, the engine had already predicted it long ago. If our students start using that engine, the situation will be worse." Laco lowered his voice, and his face still looked concerned.

They looked at each other.

"But nobody knows what it is. No, my students won't use it." Dean made a cautious statement.

"The girl stayed here for a month, sir. She has got friends here. They might be promoting it."

"Oh boy, what do we do? Should I call IT to ban 'The Flipside Cult'?"

"That's a great idea." Laco laughed and came out of the room.

In an hour, a notice was put that 'The Flipside Cult' was a corrupt site and had been blocked. Anyone accessing it, even with a VPN or proxy, would be punished.

Outside the university, Laco saw a student smoking a cigarette.

"Hey yo! Would you mind standing by the notice board, and

whoever asks what 'The Flipside Cult' is, tell them that that is where the documentary is."

"And what would I get?"

"A pack of cigarettes." Laco smiled.

With the motivation of the cigarettes, the guy told almost 100 students, and the students knew where they needed to go to get the documentary. The documentary had become a topic of discussion at the university, but nobody was able to find it on the internet. Now, little wit of Laco was enough to publicize the engine. It was banned in the university, but there was a big world out there in Congo to access the internet and 'The Flipside Cult'. All it needed was a little push and awareness about the engine.

7

The Garden of Rebellion

The courtroom was full during the fourth hearing, and there were people who stood behind, too, to attend the hearing, indicating the rising popularity of The Flipside Cult. Advocate Salem came along with the GCI chairman. The two guys could be easily spotted in the crowd. Both wore black suits and blue ties, the same height, and were wearing glasses.

Arjun reached an hour before with Veera. Apanna had not been granted bail.

Adil Salem started the proceedings as soon as Justice Singh took the seat.

"The Grain Corporation of India is the biggest supply chain management in Asia, My Lord, helping crores of Indian farmers sell their grain. Since its establishment in 1965, farmers have trusted this institute to sell their crops and get compensated for it. The GCI not only procures the grain but also helps distribute the grain with a government subsidy to end consumers and hence controls the open market price. The engine manipulates all the information and claims the GCI is not a government's instrument to help the farmers, but to appease the poor and keep running the PDS (Public Distribution System) to win the faith of the poor in India, ultimately to keep running the political wheel based on poverty. GCI is a part of a game being played by the government." He had a sarcastic laugh, took a bottle of water, and gulped it all.

"A game by the government, My Lord?" he moved towards the judge.

"The corporation has celebrated its golden jubilee, serving the farmers and the poor people across India. Had it not been for the fair price shops across the country, poor people would have starved, and the market price of grains would have skyrocketed. This is the GCI making procurement and distribution across the country, and keeping the country running. The engine is misleading the public with its faulty interpretations. The engine has blamed the government once, claiming the army as its tool, and it is again trying to tear down the nation's belief in its democratic values. This is purely anti-national and should not be taken lightly. The engine should not only be banned but also removed from the servers, with all content related to it destroyed. Our young folks here, the founding team of 'The Flipside Cult', who are working as sociopaths, should be sentenced to jail to make them understand that that is the beauty of this society, which they are projecting as ugly and a by-product of consumerism. This society is intolerant of sociopathic values." Salem showed no mercy today.

"Does this guy always talk in extremes?" asked Veera to Arjun.

"Generally, he is reasonable and very good with facts. But his tricks have not been paying him, and maybe that's why he is getting pissed off," replied Arjun in a low voice.

"Dude, he is trying to give his best. You see, he is wearing the same suit as the GCI chairman. He is trying to place himself in the chairman's position, hypothetically, so that he is more into GCI during court hearings, and bring his best out. Just to be psychologically more involved. He is desperate," said Veera while chewing gum.

"I urge the court not to consider any further requests and immediately ban the engine forever. Thank you." Salem took his seat.

"Mr. Arjun, please proceed with the defense." Justice Singh looked unaffected by Salem's intense speech.

"Your Honor, as Advocate Salem mentioned, the GCI has been serving in the country for long and has celebrated its golden jubilee. But as a citizen, I would never want an organization like the GCI to stay for this long in a system. The GCI is an indication of the fact that the country is still poor and the farmers are still relying on government subsidies. This is not about the largest supply chain system in Asia that we should be proud of, but about the policies to have this kind of poor supply chain, we should be ashamed of." Arjun too went extreme in the arguments this time.

"Objection, My Lord. I can file an additional *manhani* case if the defendant, Mr. Arjun, keeps on talking ill about the GCI." Salem almost jumped from the seat.

"This is not a public statement, Advocate Salem. This is a court hearing. Please maintain decorum. Objection overruled."

"Thank you, My Lord. Before I proceed to the engine's conclusion, let's dive deep into the two systems in India: GCI procurement and PDS (Public Distribution Shop). The PDS has been functioning since before independence, but it was revamped in the early 60s, with the green revolution. It was to ensure a subsidized supply of grain to the poor people of the country. Poor people, who made up about 80 percent of India's population, were happy about it. It was a good political move. Later, the GCI was formed in 1965 to ensure the procurement from poor farmers. An MSP was assured in case a tragedy happened. The PDS and GCI were closely interlocked. One system complemented the other. Poor farmers grew and sold to the GCI, and the GCI, with the means of the PDS, made sure that the grain reached poor people. In brief, it was a supply chain from poor suppliers to poor consumers. Poor suppliers remained poor because the consumers were also poor. Another way to look at it is, it was a wheat price regulatory move by the government. The government MSP was the price regulator. If the global vs domestic prices are compared, India offers very little price on wheat purchase. Had it been in the free market, without any regulation, the prices would have been better. India's GDP has grown since the 1960s, and there are very less number of people compared to that time who need subsidies. Still, the truth is that most of the wheat produced by farmers is procured by the government, which is stored in GCI premises, and an oversupply is done to PDS, where the wheat is sold in black markets at less than the market price. Sometimes, excess wheat rots in the GCI premises. Why has the government still maintained this whole supply chain to the same extent? This whole setup was established to be removed at the right time. But the government sees it as a price regulatory setup. The idea is to make sure that farmers remain poor! The government advertised the PDS scheme as the biggest subsidy scheme to gain the faith of the poor. Isn't it a game, My Lord? After these many years of independence, why does this still exist? This is an excellent vote machine for the government, a badly productive source of income to farmers, and a *langar (bhandara)* for poor people.

Let me take a case on ICT to explain it better. Let's consider the government as the consumer and GCI as the provider. The entities mutually related to them are farmers, wheat price, open market, political parties, BPL people, etc. Let's take a farmer, for example. The government, being a consumer, would like to get as much farm production as it can at a minimal price. GCI would be the point of sale for farmers, and for the government, it's a means to regulate the prices. Another example would be BPL people. The government would like to sell them as much as possible to gain maximum revenue; more people, more revenue. PDS would be a great way to do that. So, in the simulation, the government, being a consumer, would like to have more farmers and more BPL people to maintain the current system.

In another example, let's make GCI a consumer. For GCI, the extreme of consumerism is to buy more on less price and sell more for an even higher price. Since the government is the provider, it would set a minimal possible MSP for farmers, and GCI would get more wheat at a minimal cost. It would sell to PDS shops at a premium price, and the government, being a provider, would provide a subsidy for that premium.

Which simulation is closer to the real picture? Well, it does not matter, as in both cases, farmers, BPL people, are the ones who ultimately make the extreme ends of the current system, one towards the supply side and another at the demand side, and both are supposed to be poor to maintain the system. Or in other words, the current system of GCI and PDS fundamentally requires poor people at both ends. It's a shame that after these many years of independence, India has not been able to make efficient systems of grain supply and demand, because the government wants them to be poor. Poor people make up the biggest workforce of our country, doing low-skilled work/labour. Irony, but the development of India is driven by its poverty. The engine ultimately settles with GCI being the consumer and the government being the provider to drive the conclusion, but it's the farmers and the BPL people who are getting exploited in each case. That's all, Your Honor." Arjun finished the sentence in a low voice and with wet eyes. Probably, poor farmers in India were Neil's first motivation to invent 'The Flipside Cult', and today, the torch bearer was Arjun, without Neil. Today's win was very important for him. He just realized that his heart was an exception to his tolerance to pain.

"Advocate Salem, anything?"

"Yes, Your Honor. This boy's remarks are anti-national. These kinds of people should be behind bars. The PDS is something in the veins of the country. India is a poor country. We need systems like the PDS and institutions like the GCI. You cannot compare apples with oranges. These folks studied in the USA and are unaware of the reality of India. Who has not starved, won't know the importance of food. Who was that guy, Neil, who invented it? Must be a child born with a silver spoon in his mouth. I leave it to you, Your Honor. But I urge you to send these folks behind bars and permanently remove the engine, whatever they call it. 'The Flipside Cult.' Thank..." Before Salem could finish his sentence, he felt a strong punch on his face and fell to the ground.

"Shame on you," he heard from somewhere and saw police taking Arjun into custody.

Today was different in the court. Arjun usually presented himself as calm and composed, but today he was emotional. Anyone saying ill about Neil today would have met the same fate.

"Mr. Arjun, please maintain the decorum of the court. Henceforth, you will not be able to present a defense. Moreover, the engine continues to function, and we will be hearing the next case in the next session.

"Two gone," said advocate Salem with a grin.

*

The students in Congo refrained from speaking about 'The Flipside Cult' publicly, but individual involvement increased. Veera noticed that the user base had been increasing day by day in Congo.

"So, we have 500 participants in the African community in the Cult. This is so great," said Arjun, patting Veera. They both stayed at Apanna's apartment. It had been two days since the last hearing and nine days since Apanna was jailed.

"Yes, this is going as per my plan, good for us." Veera smiled while making a blueberry shake.

"You know, Arjun, Salem actually provoked you the other day." Veera looked right into his eyes.

"I know, but it was about Neil, and Apanna is also in jail, which makes me so stressed at times. I know he wants to get all of us off the court hearing, and he knows no lawyer would take it up. But we all got our emotional breakdown points, Veera," said anxious Arjun, settling him on the recliner outside the kitchen.

"I know, Arjun. It's all right," consoled Veera, handing over the glass of blueberry shake she just made, looking at the message she just got on her phone.

"By the way, one good news. Apanna is getting released tomorrow, just after the next hearing." Veera's eyes shone like a light bulb.

Arjun saw a strange confidence in Veera today. The other day, when Apanna was nervous about nobody taking up the case for The Flipside Cult, he remained strong and took charge, but today, he was on the other side of the table, and Veera was standing like a strong pillar in support. Veera always surprised him with her composure and her art of dealing with people. Sure, he was prompt in taking action, but Veera was next level in creating a big impact, using the available tools, including planning and execution. Every diamond has its making story, and so did Veera, the story that tells how an arrogant teenager turned into a kind and passionate person, overnight!

*

In her childhood, Veera used to stand on her balcony, holding the steel railing of their 3 BHK apartment, which her parents bought on her sixth birthday. Veera would come to the balcony every morning to enjoy the view of the rising sun in the open sky.

The area was in the outskirts of Chennai where industries started replacing the forest and people working in those industries started buying residential properties nearby. Initially, the area was a slum where factory laborers lived, but with the time it was converted into posh residential area.

"What have you drawn, Veera? Show me," her mother said to an eight-year-old Veera while wiping dust off the table.

Veera smiled and raised the sketch book for her mother to have a glimpse at.

"What are these big bars? Jail? Oh, these are the grills on the balcony." Her mother's eyes almost shone as she took a look at the innocent face staring at her.

"And let me see, this is the empty area outside the balcony, then all this green is trees, and we have got some sparrows, I guess, and finally the sun." Veera's mother almost made a song out of it.

"Sweety, is it your father looking at you while coming from a walk and waving from the ground?" Her mother sat down and asked with concern. There was a man Veera drew in her book, staring at her from the ground.

"No, that's someone I don't know, but he waves at me every day."

"Every day? Why did you not tell me?"

"Is there any problem, Mother? I don't wave back at him. I promise."

"Good girl." Veera's mother was still worried.

Veera made sketches every Sunday. One day, the sketch flew down from the balcony and landed near the man, who used to wave at Veera. He picked it. He saw it and did not appear after that. The concerns raised by her mother earlier about the man, and now his sudden disappearance, left a fear of the unknown in an eight-year-old child, forever. This incident brought a strange fear of men to Veera. Except for her father, she barely found herself comfortable in any other man's company.

Veera's sketching continued until she was 10 years old. She stored all her sketches in a box and kept it under her bed. When she turned 12 and did not see any worth in keeping the sketches, she decided to burn all the sketches. There were around 100 sketches. Before burning, she thought of having a final glimpse at those sketches. Doing so, she noticed that in two years, it was not just the man who disappeared, but also the green area, which was replaced first by olive green concrete, then with white putty. This revelation led her to realize how insensitive the world had been to its own environment. This was not just about the sparrows who lived in the green but about the whole world. That day, she ran to a cyber café and searched for environmental tragedies in the past. She also read about some famous environmental activists, and she decided that she would be dedicating her life to preserving nature.

Later in her school, Veera, who spent most of her time with girls because she was not comfortable with men, started participating in field activities related to environment in the SUPW subject, where most of the volunteers were boys. Working with boys still scared her, but she continued anyway as she was passionate about environment-related activities, i.e., cleaning the lake nearby, planting trees, etc. The more she did for the environment, the happier and more satisfied she felt.

"We need four volunteers. How come there are only three... Oh, wait, there is one more. I almost ignored her," said a boy shoveling the ground for the plantation.

Not just the group of three boys, but everybody who heard the statement laughed.

"Listen, you sexist, misogynist punk! If I hear one more word coming out of your foul mouth, I swear to Maa Kali, I will shovel your head right off and plant it underground. Not even a word, just keep on doing your work." Veera threw her watering cane away and threatened the guy, her finger pointing right to his nose. Even Veera was unsure of this sudden burst of emotions!

After that incident, no boy dared to bully her.

She understood at a very young age that life was not going to be easy for her. Society had been driven by men, and her hollow fear of them was going to pose challenges to her. But Veera learned a way to survive—become apathetic to human society. She believed that humans made a selfish society, and it was for her own good that she should keep herself away from it. Veera just worked for herself and her purpose—the environment and her academics. She seldom read the newspaper or took an interest in family functions. Behind her back, her friends used to call her arrogant. She was indifferent to society until one day she understood that society was the reason she was able to survive!

When she was 14, one day, she was searching for her old sketches, which her mother had taken from her. She searched under the bed and in the almirah and cupboards. Nothing was there. Ultimately, she lifted the mattress and found a poly-bag there, which clearly did not have her sketches, but from the transparent pink polybag, she could see a file with her name written on the cover.

'Veera.' There was no Ganesan in the title. She opened the file, and for the next two minutes, she could not feel her legs and felt like there was no ground under her feet. She sat on the bed and lay down. She found out that she was adopted. She collected her strength and came to her room.

Almost a month passed, and anger persisted in Veera's mind. Who was she? Why did those two souls bring a girl child into their lives? How was she supposed to live that harshest truth? Anger brought her headaches, and once, when it became unbearable, she decided to go to her parents and talk about it. While crossing the kitchen, where her mother spent most of her time, she saw a picture of Lord Krishna and Mother Yashoda. Picture of 'Balgopal', as her mother called it. A realization converted her anger into gratefulness. Krishna was also raised as an adopted child, but the difference he made in people's lives was amazing. It brought her faith in people. How lucky she was to have parents like them. Had she not found the papers, she would have never realized that she was an adopted child; such was the love of her parents. She went back to her room and looked at herself in the mirror. She was one of the luckiest, who was not bound by any blood relation but a relation of love and gratefulness. And how great her parents were for not adopting a male child! Tears rolled down her cheeks, and her confidence in humanity was restored. After that, she never complained about society. Dystopian ideologies might have spoiled it, but there was still hope in society that believed in flourishing help instead of competition, love instead of jealousy, and kindness instead of suppression.

*

She joined BITS for her undergraduate studies. While other students were worried about getting into student clubs and departments, which would look fancy on their resumes, Veera chose REC (Renewable Energy Club) at BITS.

"How do you think problems like climate change, global warming, and drinking water scarcity can be handled? What policies should the government be applying?" asked a member of the REC club to Veera while having a walk with her in the temple lawns during the recruitment phase. Veera was the first one to reach REC for recruitment.

"I guess it's less about policies and more about accountability. If everyone is aware of their duties to the environment, I guess the big problems will be effectively handled." Veera was quick to answer.

"You mean people are hostile to the environment, and they need to show some mercy?" the senior replied sarcastically.

"Their activities are directly or indirectly being hostile, but they just need to be aware of it. I feel that most people harm the environment because of ignorance." Veera looked at the senior and replied.

"Isn't the government supposed to take the initiative for awareness? We elect the government and pay taxes to make sure that we don't die of global warming, at least, don't you think?" the senior replied whimsically to Veera.

"You are right. But you know what? The government is governed by laws, and changing/implementing laws in parliament is a tedious process. The parliament is like a deaf old wise man. The louder you speak, the better he will respond. So, to make them realize what Mother Nature is suffering, we need voices, people's voices that can be loud and make them make some changes in the constitutional laws, but again, you see, changes start with people."

"So, this deaf wise man analogy, people accountability, and starting a people movement to make the constitutional laws appeared to you just now after our talk, or have you been involved in such activities before?" asked the senior. They reached the same place where they had started after a round.

"In school, we started a campaign, which cut down the local paper consumption by 80 percent; it should be 100 percent by next year, and many other schools have also started adopting a similar strategy in Chennai. When the state government distributed free laptops to students, as their election candy, a student group led by me proposed to use them as both textbooks and notebooks. The principal agreed luckily.

"Luckily?"

"Actually, she was about to retire the next year and wanted to have the best principal award before retirement," said Veera, laughing.

"Did she get the award?" The senior smiled.

"Yes, indeed she did."

"Girl, tell me the whole story, every bit of it. It sounds interesting. Maybe we can implement it here in BITS too.

"Sure, I do have plans for that." Veera smiled.

"Actually, books can easily be moved to digital media, but

the problem is with notebooks. In school, teachers assign homework, and they check the notebook in class. At the end of the year, the notebooks are thrown away into the trash. The learning and teaching can happen with digital notebooks, too, especially when the students are in their teens. Computer classes are a must now; everybody knows how to use a computer. So, we set up a meeting with teachers, and a committee was formed. We got it signed from every student that if found indulging in plagiarism, they would be rusticated. There are many online software available to check for plagiarism. Everybody signed. Slowly, people got familiar with it, and it was more convenient too. With Google universally available, many skills have gone obsolete. Why cling to those? Everything worked as planned." She locked her hands as she finished.

"Veera, I hope we can pull it off here in BITS too. Thanks for your time, let's connect later." The senior shook hands with her firmly.

*

It had been two years, and Veera became famous for her frequent environment-related volunteering at BITS. It was 22nd April, and heatwaves had already started almost a month ago. Veera managed to invite Mark Ruffalo (Hulk) on Embryo's (a club that organized external talks) online talk. The idea of listening to and speaking with '*The Hulk*' live prompted BITSians to leave their room and come all the way from their hostels to the LTC (Lecture Theatre Complex) under the scorching sun to attend the talk.

"Hello, guys." Mark waved from the big screen in the hall.

Students hooted and continued hooting for another minute. Mark was on the big screen wearing a green T-shirt.

"Well, guys, guys, you know why I am wearing a green t-shirt." Mark almost blushed.

A loud laughter came from the students' side, and then shouts and claps.

"Hulk... Hulk... We need hulk..."

"Ok, guys, I know you love the Hulk; I love him too. But..." He stopped and gave a smile as the students continued shouting for Hulk.

"Ok, guys, yes, I love the Hulk, and he is green, but today I am wearing green for a purpose. We love green. We all love green. I was very happy that Veera approached me as an aware global citizen. She asked me to come online and talk about how we can all contribute to solving the bigger problems on Earth. Certainly, planting trees, saving water, we can do all these, and the newer generation, even in developing countries, are becoming aware of the serious consequences of a polluted environment. Going a little bit away from the mass media environmental activities, which you can see in daily newspapers, I want to show you something that might really help to save the Earth on a bigger scale. Tell me if you plant a tree today and don't nurture it tomorrow, will it survive? If you save water today but consume more tomorrow, is it going to deliver results? You need to be accountable for the environment. Do you know the stuff you use, where it comes from, and where it goes? For most of us, it comes from the supermarket and goes into the trash. But there is a story behind every material we consume, which I am going to show you in this amazing documentary 'The Story of Stuff'."

The documentary started with the same question: where does the stuff come from, and where does it go? For most of us, it comes from the supermarket and goes into the trash, but there is a lot to it. It concluded that the current consumerism is part of a linear system, which would not sustain; we need to make it a closed loop. The key is to avoid overconsumption.

"Clicked to your engineering mind, guys? It better should," commented Mark after the documentary.

Mark had an hour-long session with the students. At the end, Veera announced a social media campaign on 'BITSians For Each Other' Facebook group, a 30-day challenge to track and reduce consumption, specific to edibles, by 30 percent. She developed an app to monitor this and shared it on the group. The first five days of consumption would be considered baseline, and the next 25 days of consumption would be tracked for a 30 percent reduction. The campaign was announced on the Facebook group with a short video from Mark, stating, "30 days, 30 percent less consumption. With each participant reaching his or her goal, I would donate $100 to an NGO working for healthcare in Africa. Let's see how much people care about other people. All the best."

Veera pulled it off. The campaign got 15,000 signups and 10,000 ended up reaching their goal. Mark sent another thank you video and also snapshot of $1M, which he donated to the NGO in Africa.

*

It was the end of her second year at college, and she was supposed to complete her Practice School 1 project in the summer. She preferred CEERI, Chennai, as she wanted to spend some time with her parents and close friends. She decided to meet someone on campus before she left.

"May I come in, Professor Anantham?" She reached the professor's office during the early office hours.

Prof. Anantham knew Veera's father and was moving to MIT US. He had an important parcel for his sister who lived in Chennai, so he called Veera.

"Hi, Veera, please come in. Take a seat. You have been an active and smart student. It's so delightful to see people your age doing things that require a great deal of courage and boldness. One of my students, Neil, moved to MIT to develop an engine centred around the forces of consumerism. In my youth, most of the youngsters worried about getting a job and settling. With improved lifestyle and standards in India. It's so good to see that young folks are not bound by myriad issues and are pursuing their passion. The young blood is finally roaring in the country. Keep it up."

Veera bid adieu to Prof. Anantham.

*

It's the end of her four years at BITS. Though she got admission offers from prestigious US universities, including MIT for her Master's, she decided to move to Chennai and live with her parents. But fate had something else written for her. Her parents died in a car accident the day she left for Chennai. The incident almost broke her from the inside. She stayed at her house and cut herself off from activism, social connections, until the day she found her sketches in her mother's room. It was put in her safe. A sudden realization of her being adopted and society as a blessing struck her like lightning. She broke her sabbatical and moved to the US for higher studies at MIT.

She cofounded 'I Wish' NGO there to offer quality social work to smart volunteers to bring an impact. There she met the most amazing person she had ever known, Neil Sengupta, about whom Prof. Anantham told her. 'The Flipside Cult' was her new identity now.

*

The lawyers for both sides changed in the following court hearing. Since Arjun was not able to defend, Veera took the plunge this time. The famous Shyam Jethramani, known for taking high-profile cases with an excellent success ratio, was representing Brilliance. Brilliance Group filed a case against the engine in response to damage to its goodwill after its local laborers, influenced by the engine's viral flipside relationship of the group with local environment, went on strike.

The space in the courtroom was not enough to accommodate the public; people could hear each other breathing while sitting there.

"Shyam Jethramani has a record of winning every case, by hook or crook," said someone in the crowd.

"He does his homework well and always finds the weak spot in the opposite lawyer," said the person sitting next to the person who spoke earlier.

"But not applicable this time. Veera is handling it for the first time. He does not know what she is going to unfold," said someone from behind in a ghostly voice.

"I think Justice Singh is supporting the engine. She knows Shyam Jethramani from a long time and his skills. She banned Arjun so that during the hearing with Jethramani, there are no loose knots. I think all of this was a plot," said a short man in a low voice.

Justice Singh entered the courtroom, bringing a stop to all murmurs.

"Please start the proceedings, Mr. Jethramani."

"Let me start the proceedings by wishing everyone here a good morning, Your Honor," said Jethramani in an elegant manner.

"The crowd here in the courtroom shows that the public is not just interested in the verdict, My Lord, but the proceedings, too, and I will try my best to bring the truth out; it's not a matter of win or lose now." Jethramani was just the opposite of Salem.

Salem was arrogant, and his agenda used to be clear in his statements. Jethramani was humble, but behind this politeness was not the respect for judicial system but a defensive shield to hide the diplomatic personality he held.

"My Lord, these young and brilliant minds, who have studied in top universities in the world, have been working for a social revolution, if I have not misunderstood them." He turned towards Arjun and Veera, sitting at the front desk.

"I also believe, theoretically, the engine does not have any fault, and probably that's the reason it's gaining massive support from the public. Certainly, these young minds are aiming for a utopian society. But to reach there, we will have to leave our current position. But the system we have adapted to is the system that would be destroyed after this revolution, if successful. We accepted capitalism, we accepted the class system. All our institutions are based on these forces. It's the question of how we have evolved economically and socially. The engine is trying to uproot the plant of consumerism and capitalism by 'enlightening people' through a digital revolution. But do they have a new seed which they can plant and flourish the society again, if not capitalism and consumerism? If people start seeing the so-called truth, which they show as a flipside relationship, they would go against the government and ultimately the entire system. Who will be there to govern the entire country if the current government falls? With over a billion people and other animals in the country, who cannot live a single day without the system in which we are, how would we support such a fundamental change? If the institutions fall, so will society. And we don't know what principles the new society would be working upon? If not consumerism, what else would it be?" Jethramni stopped for a water break.

"My Lord, every truth is not to be spoken. What they show may be right in a sense, but it's not only irrelevant but destructive. Coming to the specifics of the case, Brilliance's stocks fell by 50 percent, laborers went on strike, and production was halted in its Krishna-Godavari basin plant. The stock market is run by people's confidence in the system. Brilliance is a publicly listed company. The public's money is at stake. Coming to the Brilliance's parent group, Brilliance Industries Limited (BIL), it paid 2.88 lakh crore rupees as tax to the government in the last financial year. It employs close to a million people across the country. If something goes wrong with Brilliance's image, the country's economy would shatter.

As I explained previously, The Flipside Cult is a threat to law and order. Any output from this is not in favor of the current system. There are some truths better not spoken. The public elects their representatives to make decisions, who looks after the law in the country. For an aggregate good, sometimes we have to sacrifice individuality; it's a basic social law. The public cannot know the nitty-gritty of everything going on. Even then, whatever it has shown about the polluting environment near the Krishna-Godavari basin, it's not the right perspective to look at things. We need industries to run the country, and waste is a key part of the industries. Where would any industry dump? Brilliance Group is a six-sigma company with minimal waste; its waste management is the best in the industry. There are many other factors polluting the environment, such as vehicles, sewage dump in the rivers, sand mines, etc., how can only Brilliance Group be responsible, My Lord? I have provided you with a report where I have mentioned several other alternatives to possible pollution agents. But again, The Flipside Cult is a threat to society. Your Honor, let's say if a person has donated all his wealth, has done good social work, and never even killed even an ant in his 99 years of life, has been awarded Padam Vibhushana, but in the 100th year of his life, he murders a church father, would the court release him clean, based on his previous good works? Similarly, the engine may be built upon top-notch technology and data, showing good perspective in many areas, but if it fails in a single area, a single time, it might create lots of problems for the system. Does it reserve the right to be out there running? Who is going to regulate that? The engine is autonomous. It's not like Google, for which there are some people answerable. It's all about an algorithm. For example, Brilliance has never been involved in damaging the environment. Everything was done as per the guidelines given by the ministry. The engine somewhere must have relied on some public information that was not reliable. My Lord, for the order of society, economy, and justice, I urge you to ban this engine forever. It is a threat to society, and if allowed, would bring down the political, social, and economic system of the nation. Thank you."

The crowd was awestruck, after all, it was Jethramani.

"Ms. Veera, please start the proceedings for the defense," said Justice Singh.

"Thank you, My Lord." Veera came forward.

She had her hair tied in a bun, and her hands were in her coat's pocket when she moved forward. She did not look nervous, but neither did she look humble or confident or aggressive or defensive. She held a straight face and to everyone's surprise, she started her part with a roaring voice.

"A very good afternoon to Madam Judge, Mr. Jethramani and his team, and all the friends sitting here, who are here out of curiosity or for moral support to either of the parties. The Flipside Cult, or 'the engine' as it is famously known in the court, shows the relationship between Brilliance Industries and the ecology nearby as that of a tree and a woodcutter. The group industries have not only converted the mass agriculture land into industrial land but have also polluted the rivers nearby to a level that the water is neither drinkable nor can be used for bathing or washing. The water toxin levels are thrice the permissible level, as per global standards. The water sample report is put on your desk, Ma'am. We see big Brilliance malls, we see Brilliance venturing into different genres of production; that's the business side of it all, glamorous. The production side of Brilliance is horrible. I will come to the part where Mr. Jethramani claimed that all the Brilliance waste management is as per the guidelines by the ministry. Now, I would like to read a survey report by a Nobel Peace Prize winner, lead environmentalist, Andre Nicolas, published on his official website, today only." Veera announced in a low voice. "I will read a portion of the report, which is relevant to the case...

Brilliance Industries Limited has been a pioneer in oil and gas extraction from the Krishna-Godavari basin. The industry is crucial to the Indian economy, but at the cost of clean air, clean water, and fertile land. The industry claims that their waste management is as per the government guidelines, but the government guidelines themselves are not up to the standard. If BIL production goes on for another 30 years, both rivers would be unable to survive their ecological system. The water animals for sure would be the first to be impacted, but the toxins would spread. Toxins would go to the land water, and from there, to plants, and then to humans and other bodies. Purification of drinking water would be expensive, as the toxin amount will be much higher, as they are water-soluble. Citizens living in the nearby areas within a 10 km radius have already started reporting cases of cancer and other mutation-related diseases. Those citizens neither work at Brilliance nor use Brilliance products. They are the free consumers of Brilliance's waste. You don't always need a woodcutter to wipe out the green belt. Brilliance proved it. The polluted water killed the jungle there, and the land has been leased to Brilliance for 100 years. It's been made into a dump yard. If the government fails to change its regulatory standard to ensure an eco-friendly industry environment, and pose them to Brilliance, too, Krishna-Godavari would be a name in history."

Veera stopped for a few seconds.

"Ma'am, this is the report by Andre Nicolas, a well-known global environmentalist. The engine predicted similar to what Andre found out. He has released the detailed reports on his website. He has a history of exposing the big players in the USA and is a recipient of the Nobel Peace Prize last year. I don't think what the engine is saying is different than what Andre has shown.

We can understand it through the ICT model also. For the engine, the common entities to both Brilliance Group and the local environment are locals living there, the water, air, local government, safety standards, employment, etc. Let's make Brilliance Group the consumer and the local environment the provider, and take water as an entity. Brilliance Group would try to exploit as much water as possible. If more waste management standards were applied in the industry, it would cost the industry a lot; instead, why not dump everything in water? Similarly, for air and land. Let's take the local people as an entity. As a consumer, Brilliance would try to take as much as possible from those locals. It is giving employment, but it is taking the money back through its hospitals. A polluted region is causing diseases ranging from stomach pain to very severe ones.

In the validation stage, it all aligns with the historical data.

The engine also compares the Indian waste management standards set by the government with global standards, and it finds out that there are also big players that have managed to keep them at a sub-standard level.

Lastly, answering Mr. Jethramani's query about the regulation of the engine and its reliability, every technology we use is patented, and top-level scientists cite those patents in their papers. You see, we have derivatives of our technology already gaining momentum. It's a blockchain-based distributed system where information would need to be verified by many users, My Lord. It's not like Google, where fake news can be viral too! Regarding what comes next after the consumerism era, it would be decided by us as a whole, My Lord. History is proof that no particular style of economy, society, or politics has lasted beyond A certain number of centuries. Changes happen gradually. You can not discard a movement just because you are not on the victim side and can not visualize what would happen next.

That's all, Your Honor. Thank you."

The hall was silent. Both sides were at their best today.

"Anything from your side, Mr. Jethramani?" asked Justice Singh.

Jethramani was in a state of shock. Nobody questioned Indian standards of waste management before, and it was his plus point, but an article from Andre would for sure bring Brilliance down. Moreover, he was not prepared as it was published the same day only.

"No, Your Honor."

"An official investigation would be done based on Andres Nicolas' report. Whether the engine has misleading data about Brilliance would be decided based on the investigation." Justice Singh finished writing on paper.

"One last thing." She addressed the assembly.

"Next hearing would be for the last case against The Flipside Cult, and if closed, final verdict would be given on the same day," she said while wrapping up her stuff, looking at her desk.

8

The Cult Stood Unshaken

Right after the hearing, Veera and Arjun came to the police station to pick up Apanna. She was released from jail, but someone else went inside—Veena Kashyap, editor of 'The Hind News'. She first resigned from 'The Hind News' and then confessed to the police that she was the one who gave information to Apanna. Apanna did not steal it.

The trio met Veena in jail.

She was behind bars but smiling.

"Don't worry, I will get out soon. You guys have more important tasks now and need to be out of the cell. People love your engine; it's time for a movement, guys," said Veena from behind the bars.

Veena, a 34-year-old woman, won awards for best editor in the country at such an early age, knew what she was up to. She was very well aware of the nature of revolutions, and her focus area during her PhD was the digital revolution. She knew that the increasing popularity of the engine was going to bring down something major. But how big it would go depended on the three soldiers out there.

"I did what I had to. No worries. But, tell me, Andre publishing report on the same day as the Brilliance hearing, was it a coincidence?" asked Veena, wiping a small drop of tears from her eyes.

Arjun and Apanna smiled and looked at Veera.

"Veera worked with Andre on some projects while in the USA. He is aware of what we are trying to do. He agreed and started the investigation as soon as our first hearing started. It's Veera's ballgame." Apanna put her arms around Veera.

"Veena, where is Rehan? I will take him with me?" Apanna asked.

"He is with his Maasi. Don't worry, Apanna. I will be out soon. It was not a big crime." Veena smiled. "Now go on."

*

"I did not know she has a child. Where is her husband?" Arjun asked while driving the car back home.

"She is a single mother, Arjun. She is not married." Apanna replied while looking out of the car.

"She is a brave woman," Arjun said in a low voice.

"By the way, Jethramani's condition today was pathetic. First, he did not know anything about Veera, so he could not do his homework on her style. His first bad luck." Arjun almost shouted.

"I must say he is a sharp guy. He knew the facts were right about Brilliance, so he did not cook up any story because he knew he would be thrashed. Rather, he attacked aggressively on the engine as a whole," Arjun continued.

"Engine, too, he did not say was wrong. Playfully, he said that even if it is right, which is being proven in every hearing, it is going to bring disorder. What a chess player he is. What he was trying to prove was that the truth should not be accepted because it might shatter the foundation of a house of cards, which our ancestors built with faulty assumptions. He tried his best to bring us down," Veera intervened.

*

In Africa, the protest against the mining mafia started from a university in Congo and spread across the neighboring countries. It was a student revolution. Revolution against the government for leasing the mineral rich land to foreign entities in high volume and low prices. They stopped attending classes in public universities and protested outside in public places.

The matter had become international and caught BBC's attention.

"Hi, this is Laco, live reporting from the university in Congo. This is the new Africa, as the students call it. As you can see, we are standing just outside the University where it all began. As most of us are calling it a student revolution, let's not get misunderstood. It's a civilian protest in which most of the protesters are students. They are not protesting against the university, but as they say, against the people who are exploiting Africa, including some foreign countries and the government, for bad laws. This is the university where it all started, and the protest has crossed the border of Congo. Nobody crossed the border physically to spread the word. It's a self-propagating revolution. Let's speak to people here." Laco moved towards a student holding a banner with a slogan written on it.

"Why are you here?"

"I love my country, and I am a part of the new Africa. We are the owners of our resources; we care about them. We won't let any outsider harm our land."

"Who are the outsiders?"

"The Chinese and the Americans, digging holes here to build a pile there."

"How do you know?"

"Yo, we have some rules in our cult. We won't tell you where we discuss, share, and meet. But let me tell you, Africa also knows how to utilize technology for communication. Now let me go."

"As you can see, these students have made a cult. This is not something random, but a part of an organized plan."

Laco looked at the place where he had given the guy a pack of cigarettes.

"It all started with a documentary, apparently shown at the university function. We don't have a video yet, but it seems like that video had something that boiled the blood of the young students. We will bring it to you soon."

*

On the last day of the hearing, the trio set out at five for an early morning ride on NH 8. Arjun on the steering wheel, Apanna reclining on the passenger seat with a book in her hand, and her legs on the dashboard. Veera lay in the backseat with her hands folded on her chest. Traffic mostly consisted of trucks and buses. *Stairway to Heaven* was playing in a low volume, and the windows were down to let the cool morning breeze pass through the car. To Apanna, who was looking outside the window, the rising sun looked bigger and copper gold instead of reddish. A new sun was about to shine with all its grandeur, to destroy the darkness in the world.

It was a dawn, the last dawn of the old world.

*

Though this was the last case against The Flipside Cult, this was the first hearing when the trio was together. Not only the courtroom, but the whole court premises were full of people. Though there was no verdict until now on any case, including Brilliance's, Mr. Jethramani's failure had spread like wildfire. The faith in the engine boosted drastically, and the Brilliance stock price had fallen again by 30 percent.

Whatever the verdict was going to be today, the idea for sure was not about to die.

Justice Singh entered the courtroom. This time, she did not ask to start the proceeding as soon as she entered. She looked at the trio for a few seconds. It was not a critique's gaze, but a motherly look as Veera could feel it.

"Please start the proceedings."

"A very warm good morning to all present here. It's good that we have all the engine founders here with us on the possible day of the verdict, except one, Neil. May his soul rest in peace." Jethramani looked towards Apanna when he mentioned Neil.

"Media is called the fourth pillar of democracy, and the engine has shown the flipside relationship between media and public as 'Media is a political weapon for brainwashing crores of Indians and manipulating the public sentiments. The engine also suggests that media is increasing consumerism via inappropriate psychological tools, i.e., cooked-up surveys without solid polling, false information, and biased debates. My Lord, the media runs on advertisements. There is nothing illegal in advertising. Regarding the cooked-up surveys and polls, there is no way any online tool can claim that, as the data is the company's copyright. It's a company's IP. Nobody can question those surveys. Every company has got their own process of collecting data. A sample lot for polling may not be the same for different media channels, resulting in different results for similar kinds of polls. Similarly, false information is illegal, and no media channel would do that. I would like the defense to explain more about this. Regarding biased debates, the engine claims that media channels are biased towards a certain political party. My Lord, media channels are closely connected with the nerve of the nation. It's not the moderator of the debate who decides the direction of the debate, but the public sentiment itself. The debaters are also human beings; they also have their own insecurities. They also gain and lose confidence in their ideologies based on current public sentiments; does it mean media channels have set up some debate? It is a faulty assumption, My Lord, and based on this assumption, Media, or specifically Primes Group, for this case, cannot be called a broker, who is immorally selling its audience to the advertisers or to some political party. The engine is functioning like a *'Bangali Baba'* whom some hopeless people have started following. Let's not allow such an entity to function openly in public. We have seen the consequences in the past. Let's not give another chance to these sociopaths. I urge you to ban the engine right away and destroy its online content. Thank you." Jethramani again nailed it. He was confident today that the engine would be banned. He took his seat and gulped a glass of water.

Justice Singh called the defense.

Apanna looked at her parents sitting in the next row. She smiled at them and came forward.

"My Lord, let me start with the same story, Arjun started the first case with, as Mr. Jethramani was not present that time. Galileo, also called the father of modern physics, supported the idea presented by Copernicus that it is not the sun that revolves around the Earth, but the opposite happens in reality. It was shattering to the religious beliefs at that time. The Church held the power, and Galileo was sentenced to death. People who were beneficiaries of power at that time laughed at Galileo and also believed that the Church's power could not be won. They accused Galileo of blasphemy. Galileo's imagination and observations were not rewarded but penalized. But ultimately, the truth won. The people who laughed at Galileo did not live to see the changed world, but their descendants did. No doubt that when people could charge a man like Galileo with blasphemy, some can call us sociopaths. But I am not going to prove whether we four are sociopaths or not, but certainly the engine is a by-product of great vision for humanity and great hard work from like-minded people.

The engine has shown the flipside relationship between the Primes Group, representing the media and the public, as explained by Mr. Jethramani. Engine suggests that polls, whether exit polls or some rating-related polls, are cooked up, there is false information presented by the engine, and debates are biased. Mr. Jethramani is right that every channel has a different sample for polling, and the result may be different. Absolutely true. That was the first level of explanation. Let's go deeper. Prime Group has its quarterly product rating, and it claims that they conduct some user polls, come up with a product rating, and make a quarterly rating list. My Lord, it is surprising, but with the last 10 quarters' data, the engine found that the product which topped the list in the survey that quarter had the highest advertisement time on the channel during that quarter. Is it a coincidence that five channels, showing five different surveys, and the product topping the list is the one that has the highest advertisement time on that channel? Something somewhere is wrong. Users might be common to all of those channels, still, the top product had to be the one that had the highest advertisement time on that channel! Isn't it a sign of a cooked-up survey, My Lord?" Apanna took a glance at Jethramani.

"Let's take one example on ICT. Let's make the Primes Group as consumer, and the public as provider. Common entities are products they advertise, political parties, news, surveys, screen time, etc. Let's take news as the entity. Primes Group, as a consumer, would want to utilize the news as much as possible for its own interest. The interest of the Primes Group lies in more screen time from the public and TRP, and they would try to make the news to gain maximum benefit. The public would just switch the channel if there were more advertisements, so the Primes Group would allocate less bandwidth for dedicated time on advertisements and more on news. But it would need revenue also, so what is the best way to earn more with fewer dedicated advertisements? Integrate the advertisements with the news! So the news would be integrated with the advertisements. Don't we call it cooked-up news and false information? During the validation stage, the engine finds a positive correlation between the historical data and the news channel being the consumers.

Similarly, for debates, too, it's a setup. From the invitees to the start of a debate to the moderators' tone to a particular debater, everything is a setup. I don't think I need to add more here." Apanna looked at the audience sitting in the court. "My Lord, I am a Forbes 30 Under 30 journalist, and I do have a fair idea how the news channels run. I would not have supported the engine if anything was wrong. In fact, when I got to know about the engine, my first investigation was based on the media industry. What I found there was surprising. The dark realities that I got to know with experience, the engine was able to list them down based on data, vast data, and an algorithm that Neil believed in. We were aware of the possible consequences. We experimented with the engine before bringing it to the public. In today's time of consumerism, people present their success stories, but we have the failure stories of our engine in the archive section. We evolved. We evolved with people's support. This is about blockchain technology. People are not only supporting us, but they are adopting a lifestyle as per personal barometer, more productive and less consumptive. I urge the court that if the possibility of a revolt against a dystopian system with unevenly distributed wealth, which might jeopardize the current system, is the reason to keep the engine banned, please take into consideration the social evolutions that have happened in the past, starting with a revolution. The court is not just about protecting the constitutional ways to keep society in order. Technology was not the same when the Constitution was written. The court also protects individual rights on moral grounds. Neil started this mission alone and worked day and night to get it right. Now there are about a million active users on the engine, and there is not even a single complaint about their findings; they are able to see the truth. That's all, My Lord. Thank you." Apanna put her hands inside her coat's pockets and sat near the duo.

All eyes were on Justice Singh.

"Before I go for the verdict, I need to validate the engine's technology. The founders need to get either a testimony or certificates from authorities in the USA, where it is registered. You are given two days. If not brought to the court, the engine will be completely banned until verification is done, and the final verdict will be given after verification. Court is ad..."

"The verdict will be today, Your Honor. I will testify to the engine's technology." An old man entered the court right before the adjournment announcement. It was Prof. Anantham.

"Please come to the witness box." Justice Singh instructed.

"I am Balakrishnana Anantham, professor at Massachusetts Institute of Technology, Massachusetts, USA, and Chairman of the IEEE International Council. Currently. I have been leading the internet decentralization project at the University for the past five years. I have known Neil, Veera, and Arjun since my time at BITS. I have served 25 years in the technology, and open-source learning and development has been my key focus area. Five years ago, Neil Sengupta came to me for help to develop a product relying on blockchain technology and internet decentralization. His idea was to use individual devices for computing and storage of information, hence avoiding the cost of keeping and computing data, and making the product publicly available. It was about a product that centrally relied on ICT (Integrated Theory of Consumerism). That time, I was skeptical. I did not approve it. Had I approved it, the funding from corporate might have been canceled for my campus projects. But I admit it today, because the engine has proved itself, and there are hundreds of papers that cite Neil's theory and technology in their papers. That time, I was afraid that the engine might jeopardize the social and economic system, the system in which we have been living comfortably for centuries. But it was a superficial and selfish conclusion. Not all are comfortable with the current system. The engine has unfolded the harsh realities hiding beneath commercialization and illusion. The system we have been living with for ages has been a system of fighters. Whoever fights well, competes well is the winner and will be at the top of the chain. But for someone to win, someone has to lose. We are no more alpha men. We don't have to fight anymore. Consumption should not be the driving factor anymore. We need a change. I support the engine, and here is the verification of the technology being used by the engine. We tested each and every bit of it in the MIT labs. It is robust, stable, scalable, and trustworthy. Not a single glitch. The man was a genius. Let's not waste his hard work. Let the engine run its show. Thank you." Prof. Anantham took a seat near Apanna.

"The verdict will be delivered in one hour. The court is adjourned for a tea break." Justice Singh announced.

*

The trio and Prof. Anantham visited the tea shop.

"Ma'am, you think the verdict is going to favor you?" asked the *chaiwala* while handing over a teacup to Apanna.

"We will know in an hour," said Veera.

"Ma'am, I told you that Justice Singh is a story lover. She loves to hear new stories. She keeps on providing dates to hear new stories, and in the end, the verdict is something we all predict." *Chaiwala* again started preparing more tea.

"Tell me, *Bhaiya*, do you remember any moment that changed your life completely? I mean, do you think such moments exist?" Prof. Anantham asked, sipping tea.

"*Ji Saab*, when I left school and started working here at this tea shop." The *chaiwala* looked at the professor with a smile and realized something was not consistent with what he said.

"Today will be a life-changing moment for all of us." Prof. Anantham finished his tea.

"Laco is calling." Veera had been waiting for his call.

"Veera, good afternoon. How is it going there?"

"The verdict will be given in one hour, counting on that. How about there? You ready for what we planned?"

"Yes, pretty much. But there is good and bad news for you. Which one first?"

"Bad one."

"The internet is banned in Congo."

"Good one?"

"The student revolution has spread across the continent. Students across the continent have started using the engine, and a revolution is on its way!"

"Laco, let's end this. Let the government take a call on the engine, does not matter for now. The mafia is exposed, and people are aware; that's all we wanted. The international media is supporting the movement there. There is a positive mass support worldwide. Africa has sympathy from the environmentalists and the world media already. When they would know that The Flipside Cult is behind the exposure, the positive support would be directed to the cult. We don't want to hide and work. We want to shout loudly and say what we are doing.

One last thing from your side, Laco. Tell BBC about the video and The Flipside Cult in about two hours."

"As you command, Ms. Veera. It was nice working with you, Ma'am. May our paths cross again. Please be in touch."

"All the best, Laco."

"All the best to you guys, too, Veera."

*

Justice Singh arrived two minutes early, and behind her was a person carrying files related to all six cases.

"Good evening, everyone," Justice Singh greeted with a friendly voice.

"It has been approximately three months. To be honest, this period has tested all the experience I gained throughout my career. The judiciary is not only bound by constitutional values, but it works on moral grounds as well. Though I was the only one authorized to attend the hearing as the judge, a lot of backend work has been done by the panel set up by His Highness, the Chief Justice of India. There were experts in psychology, sociology, economics, philosophy, history, anthropology, and the Indian constitution to microscopically analyse the findings. The engine had been allowed for public use to observe its consequences, and three months is a good enough time to judge its performance. Today when we have reports about the robustness and technology of the engine. The investigation is over from the panel, and the final verdict is ready. Since it was not about winning or losing these individual cases, I will briefly summarize each case and provide the verdict in the end.

The first case was about the Indian army being used as a tool by the Government of India. The facts were found correct, and the court does not find any fault in the conclusion derived from those. But generalizing based on some instances does not make sense. We are proud of our army, and malpractice by certain government officials should not spoil the image of the whole institution. The court instructs the engine to define a certain threshold to arrive at a particular decision and comply with that.

In the second case, the court is convinced by the data and conclusion of The Flipside Cult, and an investigation committee has been set up by the CBI to look at the malpractices exercised by the NHCI for project allocation.

The third case was about loan default and public money being looted in an institutionalized way by defaulters. The court finds the facts and conclusions to be flawless, and a committee has been set up to validate the financials shown by the engine and the defense. If found guilty, the public banks would be liable for the loss, and any manipulation to recover money from the public in an institutionalized way will be dealt with strict laws. A new law will be proposed to deal with defaulters and save public money after consulting with the finance ministry.

In the fourth case with the GCI, there were no flaws in the data. Though the conclusion is misleading. Not all farmers sell the crop on MSP, and not all crops deal with the MSP condition every year. The court agrees that the GCI and PDS are in synergy and exist because of each other. The court guides the engine to define a threshold to reach a conclusion.

In the fifth case, there is no flaw in either the data or the conclusion, but the court also does not find Brilliance to be violating any national standards. But the court finds the standard to be poor in our country. A committee is already set up to investigate the poor standards, and would highly recommend adapting to standards recommended by authorized global institutions. If Brilliance is found to be involved in lobbying, as shown in the engine, strict actions will be taken.

In the sixth case, the court asks the Primes Group to submit the survey data and the source details to the court. The court will make sure that data privacy is taken care of. As consulted with the department of telecommunications, in the future, media channels are required to submit the data to the telecom department before showing the results on their channel. The engine data and conclusion are flawless."

Justice Singh did not even realize that she had been talking for half an hour. She took a sip of water and looked at the curious faces of the trio.

"Coming to the engine. As I have communicated, there are certain action items for the engine to take care of. The engine is supposed to submit the enhancement report within three months." Justice Singh stopped for a while.

"So, for three months, the engine will remain partially banned?" someone blurted from the audience.

"Before coming to that, whether the engine will remain banned or not, let me give my thoughts about what I have been hearing in this court for about three months. Now, since the technology is testified by the IEEE Global Chairman, there is no point in doubting that. Let me give my thoughts on the philosophy part. A 24-year-old visionary worked day and night to bring out such a product, which is based on flawless technology and a theory that he himself invented. The motive is pretty much clear here: a genuine interest in philanthropy. No doubt about the motive and the genius of that person. The team here is a bunch of people who could have landed hotshot jobs, earning fat packages and living luxurious lives. They left it all for a vision. I appreciate their effort and the humanitarian work. I call the engine humanitarian because it is. We have been living in a dystopian society that legalizes the uneven distribution of resources. The whole motive is more and more consumption. I won't repeat the beautiful statements made in the court by the trio about the consumption culture we have adapted to. The court understands that the engine might jeopardize the order in society, but the awareness and value it brings regarding individual freedom surpass those. The ban on the engine is lifted with immediate effect. The engine will be fully functional, unless proven guilty. Any future cases against the engine would be taken internally, and the engine won't be banned during the trial. The court wishes very well to the founders and hopes they will continue the good work. The cases are closed; the engine is free." Justice Singh spoke like it was a personal victory for her.

People clapped, and the trio almost cried. The dusk was coming to an end, and a new dawn was waiting with Neil shining in the sky.

*

"This is BBC reporting. The student revolution in Africa, which has received support from all across the world, has been found to be initiated by a search engine called 'The Flipside Cult'. The engine was banned in India after its alleged involvement in inciting the public against the country's economy, followed by a stock market crash. The engine was facing six charges filed by top government and private entities. This is a coincidence that today, when the engine was exposed to intrigue student movement in Africa, the engine won all the cases and its ban has been lifted. A video that shows how MNCs have been exploiting Africa was made by one of the engine co-founders and shown at a university conference in Congo. It was not telecast and was exclusively available on the engine, as confirmed by our local BBC reporter Laco Hossaini. The students are not only protesting the MNCs in Africa but also refusing jobs. This shows their genuine concern to save their land. Poverty-driven Africa is standing against exploitation. If you want to support them, join our campaign at the link below. If you want to know more about 'The Flipside Cult', please click on the link on the top right."

*

The trio celebrated the victory day at Apanna's apartment. 'The Flipside Cult' had become the world's voice with two historic events happening on the same day. What made this more special was that it was Neil's 25th birthday on 31st October, 2028. While talking about the cult and future strategy, suddenly a mail popped up on the phone screen of all of them, titled

'Goodbye to dystopian world' from Neil Sengupta.

Dear Arjun, Veera, and Apanna,

I am drafting this letter today on my grandmother's birthday, and I have timed it to be delivered on my 25th birthday. I will keep on updating this until I can. Since you are reading this, it means I have already left this world. Consider it the last communication from me. The end moments are harsh, and there is no time to think and speak much to express the last goodbye. I never revealed my cancer to any of you initially, but Arjun got to know. But when we had things to rejoice—our engine—why bring up something about which nothing could be done. So, I kept it to myself, my little secret, and believe me, I have lived a fulfilling and meaningful life with you guys. Could not have asked for more.

A woman's presence in a man's life makes it rich. Except for my grandmother, it's you, Apanna, who made me feel the warmth of a woman's Midas touch. I know my balance sheet is skewed in terms of caring and hurting you. But you have always been there with your arms wide open. You credit me for bringing the outspoken woman out of you, but you mesmerized me with your rare mix of love, compassion, and kindness. Thank you for always being there.

Arjun, 'a man of action', salute to you, buddy. My partner in all crimes! I never thought such a man existed in the world. Here is a secret—many times in China at 'Karma Cult', I thought to put a bedsheet over you and beat the shit out of you. But I knew you didn't feel any pain, so every time the plan was canceled. There is nothing hidden from you. Just be as you are. You will be my best friend forever!

Veera, you are a book. The more I read, the more it reveals. We all know each other VERY WELL, but then there are individual perceptions. I never knew what you were going to do next. Be it code or environmental activities or related to the engine, you always have out-of-the-box solutions for every problem! Your mental sharpness did not compete with your kindness; that's a big achievement, I feel, and you have been carrying it since your school days. Blessed to have a friend and companion like you!

I called it a communication, but communication is not complete without a response. Guys, you cannot even imagine how much I wanted to sit with you all and spend my last days with you, but things related to the engine had started gaining momentum, and unfortunately, my cancer worsened during the same time. I had things to finish, and so did you. Hopes should always be prioritized over pain, in discussions as well as in actions. 'A war against ourselves—The Flipside Cult', what a brilliant piece of article!

Guys, a question would be asked, ultimately, if not consumerisation, what else? The answer would be—community, free will, and equality, which would ultimately give a sense of freedom to us and would be the base of the utopian society. I have documented this theory and developed the free will feature in the engine. Details are there on the engine admin page when you log in from my account; documents are attached in this email.

When the time comes, we need to enable this feature to reach a utopian society.

Following is my lifelong wisdom, which has kept me moving and has always guided me:

"The roar of goodness should always be louder than the cacophony of evil."

Let's be better humans, every moment. Choice is always about right or wrong; everything else is just a story.

Always with you,

Neil

What a poetic moment it was to join Neil in the victory with his last message!

9

The Utopian Era

Irony of fate, the US federal bank announced its bankruptcy a couple of weeks after the verdict day. The faith on which the dollar was backed vanished like a house of cards. After the engine's exposure of the possible solvency of the US Fed, due to a lack of gold backup. Companies that won the faith of investors, showing their huge cash reserves in banks, hit bottom. Billionaires as well as the poorest lost all value attached to currency reserve, the only possession left worthwhile being physical assets. All financial institutions became meaningless over an announcement. The wheel just stopped running. Though all the global media were unanimous in the opinion that the Dollar value had been inflated for years, and the bubble was going to burst sooner or later.

*

The World Wide Web of internet was broken to small internets. The technology on which The Flipside Cult was built on, was no more available and hence, there was no more The Flipside Cult. The joy of celebration came with an expiry date to the trio but it did not end the hope they still carried for a better world.

Apanna turned on the TV for the news in her apartment. It was the day after the solvency of the Federal Reserve.

"All the countries are in retaliation mode. Most of the countries have banned imports and exports until further stability occurs. And no international trips are allowed as per the UN guidelines," Apanna said.

"The Republic of Congo is very dependent on food imports." Veera suddenly looked at the TV screen, hearing Apanna.

"There are more than 30 such countries in the world with food insecurity. They need to import food to survive," Apanna said.

"Let's see if the Indian government is responding to this situation?" Veera said.

"The Indian government is more concerned about the domestic crash. BSE has announced that markets will be closed until further notice. PM has consoled the public—*Bhaiyon aur beheno, sab thik ho jayega, shanti banaye rakho*," Arjun said in a sarcastic voice.

"The engine was meant to expose the faults of the current system, and now the current system itself has crashed. Now, the faulty system itself is not there. Did Neil die for this? To develop a tool that would be irrelevant after a few weeks of his departure. My head is burning," Apanna said in a panicked voice.

"No, Apanna. You are wrong. One hundred percent. The fall of the current system is testimony to our philosophy. Look at it this way, our engine got the world's eyes before the whole system crashed. What we showed has become a reality now. We have a new feature to build a new society. The universe is with us. It has already guided the path. People would trust us. If not all people, then at least a few will help us propagate the word.

Don't you think?"

"A betrayal of faith can only be healed by another faith. Let's make sure this faith does not hurt in the long run." Arjun's eyes gleamed when he said.

*

It was the sixth month after the US made its announcement, and the world became an orphan. The so-called saviors disappeared along with the dollar.

'The Flipside Cult' became the martyr, who fought for the community and died fighting. 'The Flipside Cult' was no more on the internet, but the name was on the tongue of people. Almost every young man in Africa and India knew what 'The Flipside Cult' was. The trio was well aware of this. Though there were some people who blamed The Flipside Cult for the current crash, it was all foreseen during the court trials. The majority took the engine as the torch bearer, only the torch bearer no more existed.

"Guys, see who is with us now." Arjun came into the dining room with a 21-year-old boy.

Veera and Apanna had never seen that boy. They just smiled over Arjun's greeting.

"He is Raghav from Pilani," Arjun said.

"Everybody heard of Raghav from Neil. Neil shared an intense bond with him. 'The Flipside Cult' might not have been there had he not been there in Neil's life. Neil made sure that he got a good education and supported him financially. He just graduated from BITS Pilani this year. But on the engine's verdict day, he decided to work with the engine."

"I want to work with you guys on The Flipside Cult," Raghav said intensely.

"You are welcome, Raghav, but the internet is not free, and

the engine is gone." Veera shrugged.

"Who said the engine? I am talking about 'The Flipside Cult'." Raghav too shrugged in response.

"What do you mean?" Asked Apanna.

"I mean, I was in touch with Neil *Bhaiya*. He asked me to meet you guys once I finish my college," Raghav said.

"Well, frankly, the engine was a medium, but the idea was awareness. Awareness of the last faulty system. Now the system is gone, and we have all the guidelines available with us to build a new society, through Neil's mail. Moreover, the engine might not be there, but its presence is known in the world. We will start a new faith—'The Flipside Cult.' We will go out and keep on adding people to that cult. It will be a rebellion." Raghav finished in one go.

"Two things. First, what makes us sure that people would follow The Flipside Cult? In India, it's easy, as before the announcement, it had the masses' eyes. But except for Africa, there is no other country that might show a keen interest in the cult. International coverage of D-Day was very short. Second, the engine is lost, and ideally, we need just the new feature to be implemented now on the new technology that the internet has moved to. It would take another six months to code the new feature, as documented in Neil's document," added Veera.

"The new feature in The Flipside Cult makes us sure that, ultimately, it's the faith in free will and equality that is going to last, and it does not matter how many years it takes. Neil envisioned it, and we believe in it. Our belief in it makes us sure that people will follow," Raghav spoke, determined.

"And our home page would be blank except one sentence—'Hope: Arriving on 1st January, 2030.'" Arjun almost jumped into Raghav's statement.

"I still think we need to make a strategy to get followers in the cult to challenge the government. Time is less." Veera's confusion was reflected on her face.

"Well, to answer you, Veera, young folks are the veins through which energy flows in the system. The young population aged between 18–40 makes up around 30 percent of the world population. If we are able to gain the faith of these folks in the cult, others won't take much time to understand what we are up to. And look at the history, all the fundamental changes in society are brought not by political will but by a democratic one. A mass revolution is a thousand times stronger than passing a bill in parliament," Arjun replied to Veera.

"Very well, while you three work on adding people to the cult, I will code the new feature. As per Neil *Bhaiya*'s documents, the new feature won't require much dynamic data, and we might not require much storage space either." Raghav smiled and concluded his talk for the day.

"So, the new feature will be ready by 1st January, 2030. Till then, we will be convincing people to join us. Like a militancy, a rebellion against the current faith. It will be a publicity of word for the cult. One person is going to add another person, and when the day arrives, people will unite for a single cause—a utopian society based on community, free will, and equality on 1st January, 2030. When that day comes, the world will be a much better place than what it was and what it is. The society based on free will and equality. And young folks will bring that change."

That was the last day all four people sat in the same room in a dystopian world.

*

Apanna took charge of India and eastern countries, Arjun

went to the west, and Veera stayed in Africa, covering the continent and the middle east to develop an underground cult, until The Flipside Cult was back online. Apanna travelled across the country, meeting college students and making them aware of the concept of a utopian society and how the new version of The Flipside Cult was going to achieve that. She made each of them understand that when launched, the engine would need a clear mass support to reach the dream of a utopian society. At present, as cult members, they needed to connect to more and more people and ask for support on 1st January, 2030, when the new version of The Flipside Cult would be born. Arjun too penetrated the student network in the USA and other European countries with the help of alumni from his alma mater, BITS. Veera already had won trust among African students, and with the help of exchange students from Africa studying in the middle east, she increased her network, and everyone joined as part of The Flipside Cult, at present underground, but to be revealed on 1st January, 2030.

Every member of the underground The Flipside Cult was supposed to add more and more people, nothing else, and wait for the right moment.

Students managed to utilize their network to win support of almost 25 percent of world population in the network. Faith in The Flipside Cult was unquestionable. It became the only hope in the era of disappointment, and people were eagerly waiting for 1st January, 2030.

*

1st January, 2030 was marked as the day which would be remembered as day of the smoothest and the most influential revolution in the world. With the current system not lucrative for anybody anymore, almost everybody came out of their homes to boycott the current system and go with the utopian idea suggested by 'The Flipside Cult'. Led by the youth around the globe, people discarded their national identities and vouched for a global village without physical boundaries.

Almost no country resisted the boycott. The governments were weak.

A new world was formed based on Neil's idea of utopia, a new government with no taxes, new citizens equal in all aspects, globally.

'The Flipside Cult: Community of Free Will and Equality.'

*

It was the New Year's Eve of 2050. Every New Year's Eve was celebrated with the convocation of students graduating that year, globally. One part of the world had it during the daytime, and the other at night. It became a ritual of the new society to start the year with convocation. The 2050 convocation was special. The students passing this year were the ones who were born after 2030. The students for whom the previous society was just in history books. On this special occasion, a panel of the founding fathers of the new society was all set to address the passing students.

Apanna — Professor of Modern Social Dynamics

Arjun — Professor of Modern Governance

Veera — Professor of Modern Ecology

Raghav — Professor of Modern Systems

There were no surnames in the new world!

*

"What changes did you make to bring the system from dystopian to utopian?" asked a student.

"Probably, she would take it," Arjun pointed to Apanna.

"Sure, would love to. Sometimes, big changes just need a

small tweak in the system, and the butterfly effect takes care of the big change. From there to here, it was just to make sure:

- Everybody gets equal opportunity.

- Everybody can exercise freedom by acting on their free will.

In the previous system, there was freedom exercised by more consumption; here, the freedom is exercised by acting on free will."

"How did you make sure everybody gets equal opportunity?" asked another student.

"As you must have read in the history books, previously children were the responsibility of their parents, but in the new system every child is sent to the community childcare centre, where they all get the same education and are brought up with no biases. Anyone can come and volunteer there. But, ideally, there is no identity to recognize one's own kids."

"So, every child has an equal opportunity to build their career since there is no head start passed over to them."

"Yes, and there is no concept of inheritance here," added Arjun.

"You can earn and build whatever wealth you want, but when you leave the world, you don't pass on the legacy, as there is no heir. All the wealth belongs to the society."

"So, you don't charge the tax while they are living, but you get their property when they die." One student almost laughed.

"Yes, the new government does not charge taxes, and people can enjoy their earnings when they live. But after they die, what use would their wealth be to them? Their kids are, anyway, a responsibility of the community. The government provides a universal basic income to all individual families. This income is not an unemployment wage, but to make sure that people feel free to do whatever they like," answered Arjun.

"Where does this wealth come from?" asked another student.

"All the previously churned out wealth gets accumulated by the government. With time government's wealth would increase as people keep on working, and the government would be resourceful enough to build infrastructure and provide basic income," answered Arjun.

"How do you make sure you get enough workforce for basic operations across the country, and people don't become lazy because of basic income?" a student from the back row asked the question.

"I would like to take it up." Apanna waved.

"Here comes the idea of constitutional duty for every individual. For basic operations, the government maintains an AI-based workforce management system, which statistically distributes the basic operations across the world among all individuals across demographics, like genders, age groups, professions, etc., who do these tasks as volunteer acts. Consider it the cost of being in a utopian society based on free will. Across different age groups, genders, the working hours of volunteering are generated by the workforce management system. The data suggests that on average, the volunteering duration is one hour a week."

"What about free will? How do we make sure everybody gets to act on their free will without any conflict?"

"Here comes the part, how do we ensure free will gets exercised for everyone. One individual might need some resource to exercise his free will, and at the same time, there is a high chance that the same resource is desired by another person to exercise his free will. Now, to whom does the government provide that resource?

Short answer is—it was not possible, but it can be made

possible if we modify the statement a little bit—'Everyone gets to exercise their free will either on time or slightly delayed.' Again, there are equality and free will algorithms in the system that decide to whom the resource should be made available, in case of any conflict. The system makes sure that there is minimal attack on individual free will for a longer duration of time." Apanna stopped and took a sip of water.

"What if the government gets corrupted?"

"For that part, Prof. Raghav will guide you." Arjun pointed to Raghav.

"Well, today we have one globally elected government body. The world is a village, and people elect the government. The best part is that there is no political party system. People elect the representatives who are responsible for passing the bills for constitutional amendments. There is no concept of a ruling party or opposition in the utopian government. The utopian constitution is fed into the central AI server, which gives direction to all executioners. Though the government is made of humans, the head of all departments is a central AI server that monitors the government for its work according to utopian principles and protects its citizens. The central AI server is very robust and can only be accessed once the majority of the government body decides to access it for any constitutional amendment. This AI server is a self-evolving machine that works in the interest of the utopian world. It has data, and based on historical patterns, it also makes suggestions to the government body for relevant constitutional amendments. Corruption in the government body is very unlikely for two reasons—one, there is no heir to someone's wealth, so the motivation for corruption is less; two, the AI server is very smart to catch the corruption, and the consequences are very bad. If caught in a corruption case, the representative would be thrown out of the government body, and there will be no universal basic income for him/her, and he/she would not be eligible for old age benefits."

"What about the criminal cases?" asked another student.

"Wow, I have been waiting for this question for so long." Veera almost laughed.

"There have been none in the last five years. The reason is that citizens have unique IDs based on their palm and retina scans. Nobody can abscond now! If a crime is reported against someone; he can no longer abscond, and even justice is not delayed. As soon as someone is blamed for a crime, there is vast data available about that person to connect the dots. No place is hidden from the justice department!" Veera said.

"One last question," said the host.

"What makes this society utopian?" asked one student.

"We'll let Neil himself answer this question. I have one recording of him, telling me his vision of a utopian world, and whatever he envisioned. This society has evolved to that. Let us hear our present from the man in the past." Raghav's emotions were visible on his face when he turned on Neil's recording.

"I dream of a world where the kind people rule. Where humans are not divided by class, and everybody gets equal opportunity. Equal opportunity to excel in life. A world where people cooperate, not compete. A world where nature is given priority and industries the last. A world where humans don't live to consume more, but to dream more and live more! A world where achieving the greatest heights in the mind is respected more than accumulating wealth. A world where nobody is deprived of basic needs. A world where the government does not cheat but is transparent and uplifts the deprived people. A world where somebody does not curse God for being alive. A world where pain is shared and joy is in excess. A world where no one dies of injustice. A world where there is an inheritance of knowledge, not money. A world where crime is not even born in human minds, and a world where humans express emotions freely. For our human brain has been domesticated by its own inventions. I dream of a world to freely wander in my own mind!"

About the Author

Raj Vijay is a storyteller, systems thinker, and product leader with a deep curiosity about how society functions beneath the surface. A graduate of BITS Pilani, Raj has spent years navigating the intersection of technology, economy, and human behavior—experiences that inform the soul of his writing.

The Flipside Cult is his debut novel, born from late-night reflections, restless questions, and a desire to challenge the narratives that often go unquestioned. Raj weaves dystopian fiction with philosophical inquiry, aiming to not just tell stories, but to awaken perspectives.

When he's not writing, Raj can be found building digital products, exploring spiritual philosophies, or dreaming about a quieter life in the farmlands of Rajasthan with his family. He lives with his wife Aditi, their daughter, and his ever-supportive mother in Bengaluru, drawing inspiration from the everyday struggles and quiet revolutions around him.

Instagram: @author_rajvijay

LinkedIn: https://www.linkedin.com/in/rajeshkvijayvargiya/